THE ACCUSED..

A DAMIEN HARRINGTON LEGAL THRILLER

RACHEL SINCLAIR

TOBANN PUBLICATIONS

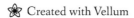

CHAPTER 1
HARPER

"WAIT, WHAT?" I asked on the phone. Damien was calling me and I couldn't really understand what he was saying. It sounded like he was telling me he was arrested for the murder of his father, but I was sure I was hearing him wrong. "Damien, I can't understand you. I must not be hearing you right."

"Harper, did you just hear me tell you I've been arrested for killing my father?"

"Yes."

"Then you're hearing me right. I'm at the station. They're trying to grill me, but I'm not talking. Please come down here. It goes without saying I want you to represent me."

"I'm leaving now," I said as I found my winter coat. It was November, and freezing outside. I had stayed late at the office yet again, as I tried to close out some files that had been sitting on my desk for far too long.

I went to my car, scraping the windshield, as it had begun to snow and I had parked my car on the street in front of my Plaza Office. I wrapped my coat around me tighter and put on my hood. I hated winters in Kansas City, even though I loved the holiday season.

As I drove towards the police station, which was downtown, so it was about a ten minute drive, my mind was racing. I had heard on the news that Josh Roland was dead, and I felt bad for Damien when I heard about it. Damien had just found out Josh was his father and was trying to give the guy the benefit of the doubt even though Josh raped his mother. I had lived through my own rape and never could forgive my rapist. Yet Damien's mother had forgiven him and Damien was trying to get to know him.

Now this. The poor guy couldn't catch a break when it came to his father.

I called the girls from my car. Abby picked up. "Yeah, Mom," she said. "What's going on?"

I took a deep breath. "Abby, I know I promised to be home for dinner tonight," I said, "but it looks like that won't happen. Better bring out that emergency pizza out of the freezer. Make sure Rina gets that essay done for her English class tomorrow and I know you have a quiz tomorrow in Algebra. Goes without saying, but the two of you need to get all your stuff done."

"Mom," Abby whined. "You promised."

"I know," I said, feeling guilty. She was right. I *did* promise to be home early that evening. They counted on me to be home when I said I would be home. I tried hard to be home on time to have dinner with them, but when I couldn't, I let them know ahead of time. They were 13, so I didn't always have to have a sitter with them. I could rely on them to either heat up a frozen pizza or order something off of GrubHub or UberEats, and I usually could rely on Abby getting her homework done and her flute practice in. Rina was usually hit or miss as far as that was concerned, but I tried to light a fire under her whenever I was around, so even her grades weren't suffering that much.

"You know, Mom, but what?" Abby demanded.

I sighed. "I have a very important client," I said. "I'll tell you about it when I see you tonight."

"Who is so important, Mom? Who is more important than your promise to us you'll be home tonight?"

"Damien," I blurted out. I didn't want to talk about this over the phone, but I figured she would find out sooner or later. "Damien is so important. He's down at the police station right now. He was arrested for killing his father." I saw the police station coming up, and I pulled into a spot on the street right in front of the building. "Now, I'm here at the station and need to get in there and see him. I'm sorry, really I am, and, believe me, if it were anybody else but Damien, I would be home right now."

Abby sighed. "I'm sorry, Mom," she said, sweet Abby returning. "I should have known you really did have an emergency. Don't worry about me and Rina. I don't really want that pizza, so I'll just order something from UberEats if you don't mind."

"Go for it, Buttercup," I said. "I'll be home as soon as I can."

"Okay." She was quiet for a few seconds. "Will he be okay? Uncle Damien?" Her voice sounded anxious.

"I don't know," I said truthfully. "I wish I did, Buttercup. I hate to say it, but I don't know any more about this whole thing than you do, which isn't much. All I know is he just called me from the station. I saw shis father was murdered, but I just couldn't imagine Damien being behind it all."

I talked to Abby as I approached the building. I went in, gave my ID to the woman behind the glass. She nodded and buzzed me into the area where I could talk to Damien.

"I'll tell Rina," Abby said. "She'll be upset."

"I know." I drew a breath. "Not to mention his kids. Oh, God, I hope they're okay. I know they have a sitter, Gretchen, but I might have to take them if Damien doesn't make bail." I shook my head. "I'll burn that bridge when I come to it. Bye, Buttercup. Have to go."

I hung up the phone and followed the officer to the interrogation room. Damien was sitting at a table, his arms crossed in front of him, glaring at the officer standing above him. I put my briefcase down on the table and sat down next to him.

"Hey, Harper," Damien said, his glare trained on the officer. "Glad you could make it."

I crossed my hands. "Okay, get me up to speed here," I said. "What's going on?"

"My father was found in his office, bludgeoned by a table lamp. There were signs of a struggle – the floor lamp in that office was knocked over and papers were strewn all over the floor. My fingerprints were apparently on the lamp base." He glared again at the officer. "Of course my fingerprints were on that lamp base. I'd been in the office and touched that lamp while I talked to my dad. I was nervous when I met him. I have a nervous tic that makes me want to touch things on people's desks. Paper weights, lamp stands, statuettes, whatever. I touch things when I don't know what to say to somebody."

I whipped out a yellow pad of paper. "Okay," I said to the officer, whose name was Officer Leeds, "you have my client's fingerprints on the lamp base. What else do you have on him? I'm listening and I don't hear anything that gives you guys probable cause to arrest him. I better hear something more than the fact that Damien's fingerprints were on the murder weapon or I'm going to demand you release him."

Officer Leeds narrowed his eyes at me. "His fingerprints were the only prints on the lamp base except for the victim's. This was a brand-new table lamp, just bought today. If there was some other person who used that lamp as a weapon, there would be some sort of other fingerprints on it. There was none."

I cleared my throat. "Well, I still don't believe you have enough evidence to hold him. It's November. Somebody could have come into the office wearing gloves and done this."

I had to admit it looked bad that only Damien's fingerprints were on the murder weapon, especially since it was a lamp. Because the lamp was used as a murder weapon, it could reasonably be assumed the murder wasn't premeditated. Therefore, it could reasonably be assumed the perpetrator wouldn't have been using rubber gloves or some other method of concealing his or her fingerprints. But it was a possibility that somebody was wearing winter gloves when he or she did this.

Either that or somebody clearly framed Damien for this. That was the only other explanation I could think of for why Damien's fingerprints were on the lamp and nobody else's fingerprints were.

"We have probable cause to arrest him because his fingerprints were on the murder weapon. You're the lawyer. You know very well that something as simple as that can be enough to charge somebody." Officer Leeds glared at Damien. "Plus, your client has not exactly been a choir boy. He has quite a juvenile record."

"A juvenile record? A juvenile record? You're using his juvenile record against him? That stuff is sealed."

"It's been unsealed," Officer Leeds said. "By the governor himself."

"Governor Weston went through the trouble of unsealing Mr. Harrington's juvenile record?" I was dumbfounded about that one. "Why would he do something like that?"

Office Leeds shrugged. "Ask Governor Weston that question. I obviously can't answer that for you. I can only state that happened. Because Governor Weston unsealed your client's record, I can also tell you that Mr. Harrington will go in front of the Missouri Bar soon. He lied on his Bar application when he said he had no adjudications. He clearly did. But that's neither here nor there."

I cocked my head at Damien, who was having a problem meeting my eyes. "Okay, well, I understand Mr. Harrington probably had some issues in his youth. I don't know what they have to do with this charge, though."

"He has a charge from when he was 15 years old. He beat up a 21-year-old guy named Julian Wise. He used brass knuckles. The guy went into the hospital for three days because of it. He has also stolen three cars. He was involved with an underground gambling operation and served as the enforcer for this underground group. Your client was lucky he was put into prison when he was 18. It seemed to have straightened him out." He looked over at Damien, who now was hanging his head down. "Seemed is the operative word."

"Well," I said, feeling at a loss for words. Inwardly, I was seething at Damien. He never told me any of these things. He told me he was wrongfully imprisoned at 18, but he never bothered to tell me about his juvenile crimes. I was completely blind-sided by this officer. "I don't think *seemed* is the operative word here. Ever since my client has lived a stellar life since being released from prison. He's highly respected in the legal community. He has no adult criminal record. Besides, you know as well as I do you can't base probable cause on a person's record. Especially a juvenile record."

"No, but we can base probable cause on the fact that your client's fingerprints were on the murder weapon and he had motive for killing Mr. Roland."

"What motive?"

"The victim raped his mother. That's your motive right there. That would be enough for Mr. Harrington to want Mr.

Roland dead, but that's not even the most compelling reason Mr. Harrington had to kill Mr. Roland."

"Oh? What other motive did my client have for killing Mr. Roland?"

"Mr. Roland had confidential information that could have sent his best friend, Nick Savante, back to prison."

CHAPTER 2

I sighed. There was one thing I knew about Damien - he would do anything to protect his best friends. I didn't think killing somebody would be in his wheelhouse, but one never knew. It depended on what Josh Roland had on his friend, Nick, and how good this piece of information was.

"What piece of information did this guy have about Nick?" I asked Officer Leeds. "That would send Nick to prison?"

"Nick is apparently already violating his parole," Officer Leeds said. "Damien got Nick a job with Mr. Roland. Damien's first mistake. He should have figured Nick would get sticky fingers. That's what allegedly happened. We have found, through our preliminary investigation, that Nick was stealing from Mr. Roland's company. He was inflating invoices and pocketing the money. Mr. Roland was on top of this. He fired him and called Mr. Harrington into his office to read him the riot act about introducing Nick to him. That was when Mr. Harrington killed Mr. Roland."

I looked over at Damien. He wasn't looking at me. Then he looked at me, shook his head and rolled his eyes. I gave him a look that told him not to speak and he got it. He shook his head again and looked away. I could see burning hatred in his eyes.

"Will Nick back to prison?" I asked Officer Leeds. "Is there an arrest warrant out for him?"

"At the moment, no, there's not, but there soon will be."

"Okay." I nodded. "Will you charge my client in his father's murder?"

"We are. He hasn't spoken to us because he knows better, being a lawyer himself, but, yes, we have enough evidence to charge him. I anticipate we will. I just need to get word from my superior about this, but I think he'll be charged by the end of the night."

I took a deep breath. "Do you mind if I have a word alone with my client?"

"No, not at all," he said. "Maybe you can talk him into doing the right thing and confess."

Damien rolled his eyes and glared at Officer Leeds as he got up and went outside the door.

I looked at the window, knowing we were being watched and listened to the entire time. Therefore, I wouldn't talk to Damien about anything of substance. "Damien," I said, "how are you holding up?"

He shrugged and said nothing.

"Well, I guess you'll be charged and booked," I said, "I'll be there for your initial appearance. I don't anticipate a problem getting bail for you."

"I don't know about that," Damien said, his voice seething. "I pissed off somebody pretty high up on the food chain. He's getting his revenge. I fully anticipate I'll be denied bail. I wouldn't be surprised if that's the case."

"Damien, it's your first offense," I said.

"No, it's not. My juvenile record has been unsealed. I have a record now, Harper, and not a great one. Plus, Harper, I'm telling you, this one goes all the way up to the top. You have a handful on your hands, Harper, a handful."

"Damien, you're not making any sense."

"I know I'm not," he said, "but I will. We just need to get to a place where you and I can speak privately. When we're not being watched through a two-way mirror. I need you see me tomorrow morning in the jail. A professional visit. I'll tell you everything."

"Okay," I said. "In the meantime, your kids..."

"Yeah. I hate to ask this of you, but do you mind taking them?"

"No, no, of course not," I said. "I'll pick up Nate and Amelia after I leave here. I'll pack a bag and bring them over to my house tonight."

"Thanks." Damien hung his head. "I have a story to tell. This whole thing reeks of a setup and I have a good idea on who's behind this. And, Harper, when you find out who's behind this, you'll be stunned. Absolutely stunned."

At that, the officer came back in. "Time's up," he said. "We're going to charge your client with the murder of his father." At that, he put the handcuffs on Damien and read him his Miranda Rights. "Mr. Harrington, you are under arrest for the murder of Joshua Roland. You have a right to remain silent..."

After they read Damien his rights, they took him out of the room to be processed. He looked back towards me as he was being marched out and I felt for him. He was 35-years-old and a well-respected attorney. He'd won some really amazing cases. But yet, here he was, looking like a scared kid. That was the look on his face – that of a terrified kid.

He knew something. I could tell. He knew something and his look told me things were dire.

Very dire.

As I left the police station, I was filled with a feeling of dread.

Something told me this case would be one of the most challenging of my entire life.

I hoped and prayed I was wrong.

CHAPTER 3

The next day, I met Damien for his initial appearance. I saw him coming out in his orange jumpsuit and my heart went out to him. I knew how humiliated he felt. I had been where he was. I was in court for my kidnapping charge back in the day when I was determined to protect my kids at all cost. I was also in court for a DWI when I was framed by the cop in the Darnell Williams case. Both times, I knew my colleagues were whispering about me behind my back. I shouldn't have cared about that, but I really did. Nobody wanted to be humiliated in front of their peers.

I went over to him and put my arm around his shoulders. "It'll be fine," I whispered. "I talked to the prosecutor and they're against giving you a bond. I'd like to talk to Ally about this, though, and see if she can pull some strings so I can get you a bond review with little opposition."

Damien shook his head. "You can try, Harper, but trust me when I tell you I won't be granted a bond. I'm being accused of murdering one of the richest men in the city. Credibly accused of murdering him, I might add. I'll be very surprised if I'm granted a bond."

"We'll see," I said. "It's worth a shot."

"I guess."

"I think we have a shot, but if you're not granted a bond, you probably need me care for Nate and Amelia. Right?"

"Right." He put his hand on my shoulder. "Harper, I wanted to tell you how much I appreciate your support." He hung his head. "Man, I'm in the middle of a nightmare. A complete nightmare." He looked at me. "Harper, I'd like you to do something else for me, if you don't mind."

"Sure, what do you need?"

"Find out what happened with Nick. I just can't believe he would violate his parole like that. I'm telling you, I think there's something rotten going on. Really rotten. I haven't quite figured it out, but I have a good feeling about what's happening. I have a feeling all the guys will be in trouble, sooner or later." He shook his head. "I've made a very powerful enemy, Harper. Nobody will be safe until you and I come up with a plan to stop this."

I was intrigued. He still didn't feel comfortable telling me everything. I knew why. He knew as well as I did that attorney-client privilege only applied when he and I were one-on-one. Anything he told me right at that point wouldn't be covered by privilege. I was therefore anxious to visit him in jail or, hopefully, at his home, assuming he could make bail.

The judge got on the bench and started to call his cases. "I'll take the inmates represented by private counsel first," he announced, and then he called several cases, all of whom pled "not guilty," before he got to our case.

"State verses Harrington," he said and then looked surprised when Damien came up to the bench. "Mr. Harrington," he began and then he shook his head. "You've been charged by the

State of Missouri in one count of Murder in the First Degree. How do you plead?"

"Not guilty, your honor," he said.

"I would like a bond review," I said. "At the moment, Mr. Harrington is held without bond. He's not a flight risk. He's also a respected member of the bar." I leaned forward. "Please, your honor. You've seen Mr. Harrington in court, time after time. He's one of us."

He shook his head and studied the file in front of him. "Let's see..." He carefully read the charges and evidence. I knew this judge, Judge Kenner, typically didn't see the file before he got on the bench for the initial appearances. There were just too many files and defendants on any given docket for him to have studied every single file beforehand. But this was Damien, one of our own. That gave him pause. "You've been charged with the murder of one our most prominent citizens, Josh Roland."

I knew his dilemma. This was a case the media was covering extensively. Josh Roland, for all his problems, was a billionaire and a prominent CEO of a major corporation. He had his issues with drugs and sexual harassment and apparently raped at least one woman, Damien's mother. But these issues were swept under the rug. Josh had a handler charged with covering up all his misdeeds, a professional whose only job was to pay off anybody who needed to be paid off or blackmailed whoever could be blackmailed, so all of Josh's crimes and misdemeanors were never covered in the newspaper.

So, for all intents and purposes, Josh Roland was an upstanding citizen. A philanthropic billionaire who funded hospital wings and had entire university halls named after him. Children's Mercy, the children's hospital that relied on philanthropic funding because it provided so much indigent care, was kept afloat because of Josh Roland's efforts. His annual charity balls for Children's Mercy were legendary and raised billions over the years. He also was a part of the investors who funded the Kansas City Chiefs. If there was one thing Kansas Citians passionately loved, it was the Super Bowl-winning Chiefs. Patrick Mahomes and the Chiefs were Gods in this town, rightfully so.

Plus, Josh Roland's firm, Aragon International, was on the cutting edge of bio-technology. While he did come from old money – his great-grandfather made his money in diamonds while his grandfather got into shipping and lumber – Josh made his own path, using his inherited fortune to found an internationally well-respected company that locally employed thousands of people.

I wasn't hopeful bail would be granted to Damien, but I had to pray this judge would see past who the victim was.

Judge Kenner looked at Steven Harper, the prosecutor assigned to this docket. "Mr. Harper, do you have any objections to Mr. Harrington being assigned bail?"

Steve looked like he was put on the spot. I knew his dilemma – Damien was a colleague, a respected member of the legal community. The criminal bar was close-knit. Prosecutors and defense attorneys were generally friendly with one another. Especially a defense attorney like Damien, who worked in the Public Defender's Office for several years, which meant he got to know almost everybody in the prosecutor's office, even Steve.

Yet Steve had a job to do.

"I do object, your honor," Steve said. "Mr. Harrington has been accused of a very serious crime. Murder One." That was all he said, however. He couldn't say much more.

"Ms. Ross," Judge Kenner said, "What say you?"

"My client is not a flight risk. He's a well-respected member of the bar and has two small children at his home. He doesn't own a passport, so there's no chance he can leave the country. I understand he's been accused of a very serious crime, but that's not a sufficient reason to deny bail to my client, your honor."

Judge Kenner studied the file some more. "Okay, here's what I'll do. I'll set bail at $3 million cash. The terms and conditions of the bail are the defendant shall not have contact with anybody working for Aragon International, he cannot leave the jurisdiction, he will be monitored electronically, he cannot leave his house unless he is going to work and he cannot have contact with known felons. I understand Mr. Harrington is an attorney, but I must restrict his movements. I'm very sorry, Mr. Harrington. I know you most likely have cases in far-flung places like Harrisonville and Bonner Springs, but, for now, I need you to stay in Kansas City proper. If you have cases in those other suburbs, I'm afraid you'll have to reassign them. I'm sorry, Mr. Harrington, but that's the best I can do."

Damien looked surprised he was getting bail. Granted, $3 million was very steep, and, in order for Damien to make that bail, he would have to drain all of his savings, but he would get out of jail. That was important.

All I could think of was that it was a great blessing Damien won that major wrongful death case. If he didn't, he probably wouldn't have had the money to get out of jail.

"Thank you, your honor," Damien said, looking at me in wonder.

The guard led him away and he looked back at me. "Meet me at my home this evening at 7," he said over his shoulder.

"I'll be there."

I left the courthouse feeling pretty good. It definitely could have been worse. Considering how important and wealthy the victim was, I was prepared that Damien would be denied bail. He wasn't, so that was a good sign.

At least I hoped it was.

CHAPTER 4

That night, I went to Damien's house, a few blocks away from my own. I had Sophia watch the girls, because I had a feeling that it would be a long night and I wanted to make sure the girls got to bed on time, did their homework and were fed. Abby wasn't very happy about the fact that I was, once again, going to be gone that night, but it couldn't be helped. He had a story to tell and I needed to get to the bottom of it.

Abby was finally getting to the point where she was becoming mouthy and rebellious. Rina had always been at that point. Rina always wanted to test me while Abby was shy, quiet and reserved. Now it seemed Abby had found her rebellious voice, so I had two identical girls constantly trying to test my authority over them.

As if my life wasn't complicated enough. But that was okay. I somehow managed to discipline both girls to where they weren't quite running the show. I white-knuckled it the whole way, but I still managed to, for the time being, stay on top of things at home.

However, I always knew it was a matter of time before

things spiraled out of control with the girls. They were at the age where they were in danger of being sucked into things young teenagers got sucked into – drinking, drugs, sex. I was drinking when I was their age. I was an alcoholic by the time I was 14. I worried, constantly, that Abby and Rina would fall prey to bad influences. It didn't help that I had so little time to stay on top of them. Sophia was great but wasn't always around and I left the girls alone far too much.

The guilt about that was overwhelming but I needed to do this for Damien. I had grown fond of him and was thinking of offering him a permanent partnership with Tammy and me. Tammy was on board for this plan, 100%. She liked Damien as much as I did. He was a good, upstanding guy who was one helluva attorney.

I needed to make sure he beat this case. I couldn't imagine any other outcome than that.

I got to his house. He saw me coming up the walk and was waiting at the door for me.

"Harper," he said, as I walked through his door. "Thank you for coming."

I nodded as he motioned to one of his easy chairs. "Where are the kids?" I asked him.

"They're in their rooms," he said. "I told them I needed to talk to you about something very important and they've made themselves scarce. They know what's going on, Harper, and they're freaked out. Completely. They know what will happen if I get convicted for this." He took a large breath. "Harper, I hate to even bring this up, but I need to. Are we still good? Are you still on board for taking guardianship of the kids if something happens to me?"

"Of course," I said. "I told you I would be there if something happened to you and I meant that. We have paperwork drawn up about that. So, yes, don't worry. I have your back if push comes to shove. Which I hope and pray it doesn't."

Damien appeared to relax slightly when I confirmed I would take his kids if he was convicted.

"Thank God," he said. "I have so much against me on this. I'd lose my mind if I had to worry about whether or not the kids would go into foster care if I get convicted."

"Well, don't worry about that. I got this." I took a deep breath. "Now that that's out of the way, you and I need to talk about how we can avoid me taking guardianship of the kids. We need to get you off this charge."

"I know. I just don't think this case will be easy to win. It's not just that my fingerprints were on the murder weapon. It's not just that I have an extensive juvenile record. It's not just that my best friends have just gotten out of the joint after serving 17 years for felony murder. There's something else you need to know."

"Go ahead." Damien obviously had a lot on his mind and needed to be unburdened. I would let him do that. "Tell me what I need to know."

Damien shook his head. "I don't know why I ever thought I could hide this from you. But I have. I've done some ethically questionable things and have also done something downright illegal. Unfortunately, the illegal thing I did involved our governor, and, I have to say, I think he's getting his payback."

"Okay. Go ahead."

He sighed. "Connor O'Brien was facing life in prison without parole. The other guys – Jack, Nick and Tommy – were all up for parole this year. You know that. They're out now. You've met them. They're great guys. But Connor was the trigger man. He actually shot that security guard. It was really an accident, Harper. He was 16 years old and panicked. He had a gun in his hand, that security guard pointed his own gun at him, and he panicked. He shot that security guard in the leg. The security guard died in the hospital from an infection. MRSA. A perfect storm, really. So many things went wrong."

"I know. I remember you telling me about all that."

"Right. Well, the other guys got life in prison with the chance of parole. I managed to get their sentences commuted when I got out of prison. I threatened that governor, Governor Steele, with exposure of all the issues that happened in my trial. I would go to the media about how the prosecutor's office with-held exculpatory evidence and coached the eyewitness to testify against me. I found many, many mistakes made, and had a very good case for a multi-million dollar lawsuit against the state. I told the governor I would drop all my claims against the State of Missouri in exchange for him commuting the guys' sentence. He said he would commute the sentence of Tommy, Nick and Jack, because they weren't the gunman in the case. But he refused to commute Connor's sentence. I took what I could get, but, trust me, I was devastated I couldn't get Connor off as well."

"That's right," I said. "Governor Steele commuted their sentences down to 20 years in prison."

"Yeah. They served 85% of their sentences and then got parole." He took a deep breath. "But that's not the entire story. There's more. Much more."

"Go on...."

"Well, it started with Nick. You remember Gina DeGrazio, right? That mob wife I defended awhile back?"

"Of course. She had that self-defense claim."

Damien shook his head. "You know, in a way, it's a good thing I was arrested for murdering my father and you're my attorney. Because I can now tell you everything and there's no way you can get into trouble for knowing these things about me. I could never tell you about this before, because I knew you would have an obligation to report me to the Missouri Bar for my ethical misconduct. But, since you're my attorney, this is covered under privilege. The privilege will supersede any ethical duty you might have to turn me in."

This sounded serious. It sounded like Damien might have done something serious in Gina's case. I wondered what it was, and I wondered how his friend Nick factored into it all. My curiosity about this was piquing. "What did you do?"

He sighed. "I had to win Gina's case. Yet I found out that Vittorio, the victim in that case, had an identical twin who killed him. Enzo DeGrazio."

"Okay. So, Enzo DeGrazio killed Vittorio, yet you went for self-defense?" Something wasn't adding up. "I don't understand."

"Boy, that's a long story. A long, complicated story. But the upshot was that Gina and Enzo had an agreement. He paid her $3 million bond and Gina was entitled to get that bond if she beat the case. She couldn't finger Enzo, however, because Enzo was tied to the mob and could and would have her killed if she brought him down."

"What am I missing here, Damien? You had the case solved, but went another way. You would had to have suborned perjury to get to the conclusion you were aiming for. Why didn't you just withdraw from the case?"

Another sigh. "Oh, where do I begin. Okay, I hope you can follow this chain, because it all gets really tangled up. Gina's lover is a guy by the name of Joey Caruso. He's serving life in prison for killing his wife. He knew Nick murdered a fellow inmate in prison. Nick had to do it because that guy, Ward Johnson, was threatening Connor's life. Ward was psychotic, according to Nick, and had delusions that Connor was actually a guy by the name of Chad Jameson, a guy diddling Ward's wife on the outside."

I nodded, knowing this was tough for Damien to tell me. I, too, was happy I was his attorney. Otherwise, I would've had an obligation to report these incidents. I would've been required to tell the authorities about what Nick did, and whatever Damien did, I would've been required to tell the authorities about that as well. But attorney-client privilege in this case meant I couldn't say one word.

"Okay, so Nick killed a man in prison, and this Joey Caruso knew about it."

"Yeah. That's right. Well, Joey was threatening to squeal on Nick if Gina didn't get acquitted. Turned out Gina owed Joey $1 million. Joey gave her $1 million so she could launder his mob money through some massage parlors. Well Gina was none too bright, so she instructed her girls to give happy endings. That caused all of the massage parlors to be shut down by the city, which meant Joey lost his investment. Well, Joey was sorely needing cash himself so he could get his son out of debt. His son was being hunted by the mob because he owed the mob $1 million."

I was having some problems following the thread. "Okay. So, Gina owed Joey $1 million and Joey needed that million to get his son out trouble. And Gina was set to keep her $3 million bond if she got acquitted so she could pay off Joey. You couldn't tell the jury the truth about Enzo, because if you did, Enzo would have had Gina killed, which would mean she couldn't pay off Joey. Right?"

"You got it. And Joey threatened that if something happened and he didn't get his million, he would rat on Nick. He made that threat so I would do all I could to get Gina acquitted. That meant, of course, I couldn't withdraw from her case. And I couldn't tell the jury the truth about what happened. So I had Gina lie and tell the jury it was self-defense. I suborned perjury."

That was bad. That was very bad. He could very well be disbarred for doing something like. Not that I could really blame him – he was in a tight spot. I supposed I would do something similar if I were in a spot like that.

"Okay, so it all worked out, then?"

"Yeah. Gina was acquitted, Joey got his money and nothing happened to Nick. And now Nick is in trouble. I still don't believe it. He'll have to find another attorney to represent him, obviously, because if the story is I killed my father because he had the goods on Nick, you obviously can't represent both him and me at the same time."

"I see," I said. "So do you think Nick being in trouble has anything at all to do with that whole Joey-Gina-Enzo mess?"

"Could be. I don't know yet. But let me tell you about something else I did. Something I think brought this whole thing on my lap. Now, before I tell you this, I have to caution you about one thing. I haven't yet worked it out in my head how everybody is involved in this. I can only tell you what happened and we can start working on a theory based on what I'm about to tell you."

"Go on."

A deep breath from Damien. "Well, I did another bad thing. My last client, Leland Dewitt, had some pretty good evidence I could use to blackmail our current governor. Apparently, our current governor, Mr. Family Values himself, likes boys. He sent a dick pic to Jackson Michaelson, the victim in Leland's case. And I might have used that dick pic to blackmail the governor into commuting Connor's sentence."

I had to suppress a laugh. It was right there, but was inappropriate, so I looked at Damien's lights in an effort to suppress it. That didn't work. I started to giggle, and, before I knew it, Damien was also laughing.

"Oh, God," I said, "I'm sorry, this really isn't that funny. It's just that..." I shook my head, still laughing, "it's just that I was thinking about how he was always crusading against marriage equality and signed all these laws that state employers can fire people just because they're gay and he's always making speeches about how gays shouldn't be allowed to adopt. He wants to protect wedding planners from the gays. And he likes boys. You really can't make that up, can you?"

Damien was also laughing. "No, you really can't. But you know what they say – the most anti-gay people are usually struggling with their own sexuality. If they were confident in their sexuality, they probably couldn't care less about what people are doing behind closed doors. At any rate, yes, our anti-gay family-values governor likes boys. I had photographic proof of it and used it. Without hesitation. I got what I wanted – Connor is out of prison – but I think I might be paying the price for it now."

I nodded. "Okay. I guess I'm not following."

"I don't really know myself," Damien said. "It's only a theory. I might just be paranoid. See, ever since I gave the governor what he wanted – the cell phone with the dick pic and the copy I made of it – I've been paranoid the governor will want revenge. If you can recall, he got some blow-back for commuting Connor's sentence. The law and order people were protesting him and he now has a primary challenge because of it. The media made that whole sentence commutation look like Governor Weston was pardoning Charlie Manson himself. Do you remember reading about all that?"

"Oh, yes, do I," I said. "That was certainly a scandal. I thought it was ridiculous the way the media portrayed it. Connor was 16 when he was involved in that robbery and certainly didn't mean to kill anyone. If he didn't shoot that security guard, the security guard would have shot him. Yet the way the media, especially right-wing talk shows, portrayed it, you would've thought Governor Weston was pardoning a serial killer."

That was the truth. All the right-wing talk show hosts were salivating over Governor Weston commuting Connor's sentence. All they told their listeners was that Governor Weston had "pardoned" - which is a wrong word, because a commutation is much different than a pardon - a cold-blooded killer. They banged on that drum for weeks on end until the governor ended up with mass protests against him and a primary challenger in the person of Cole Tobias. Cole was a farmer from the boot heel raised by his "God-fearing Aunt," who firmly believed murderers like Connor needed to not just die in prison but die with a needle in their arm. Cole had seized on that one issue to launch a grass-roots primary challenge, and, the last I saw, he was leading in the polls.

"Yeah. So, I put Governor Weston in a bad position. I told him that if he didn't commute Connor's sentence, I would hand over that cell phone to the authorities and tell them the penis in that picture belonged to him. That would have ended his career in scandal. So he commuted Connor's sentence to avoid the dick-pic scandal, only to land in a bigger scandal by this whole commutation thing blowing up in his face. I have a feeling Governor Weston is good and pissed at me right about now."

"Yes," I agreed, "I would imagine so. I mean, before Connor's commutation, he was a popular governor cruising to re-election. Now he's fighting off a primary challenger and the right-wing talk show hosts are still bagging on him for the Connor thing. He could very well lose his governorship because of it." I paused. "But what does any of that have to do with this?"

"I don't know," Damien said. "I'm only throwing it out there for you just because I wanted you to know the bad things I've done. Either one of those bad things could be why I'm in this position right now."

"Well," I said, "if you think the governor had Josh Roland killed just to frame you, that makes little sense. It would be much more efficient just to have you killed, wouldn't it? And why would the governor have something against Josh? Josh was a Republican and, from what I've gathered, was one of Governor Weston's major donors. I don't think Josh abandoned Governor Weston after the Connor thing, either. He wasn't supporting Cole against Governor Weston."

"As I said, I don't know," Damien said. "I've been trying to put it together. This whole thing is in my head, and, you're right, I'm probably just paranoid. After all, I was convinced I would have been denied bail today. I thought the governor would have gotten to the judge and forced him to deny me bail. That didn't happen. So maybe I'm wrong about all this."

"Well, it's food for thought," I said. "Definitely. But would the governor also be behind framing Nick for embezzlement? Or maybe that was somebody else? And you're sure Nick isn't good for that crime?"

"I'm not sure about anything. I wouldn't imagine he would be, though. He and the guys have been doing well. Tommy is working with Garrett, doing private investigator work, and Jack has a good job in construction. Connor has been accepted into the UMKC program for social workers because he wants to help people like him choose a better path. And Nick was working with Josh as an assistant. Now, Nick is in trouble, Josh is dead and I'm accused of killing Josh, my own father."

"So, you think it's possible Nick would do something like that? Embezzle?"

"Harper, anything is possible. Probable, no. Nick knows he has a second chance and knows he has it much better on the outside than do most of his fellow parolees. Josh was paying him an okay salary - $15 an hour – so Nick really didn't have to steal from the company to make ends meet. Yeah, it's not a fortune, $15 an hour, but he lives with Tommy in a two-bedroom apartment that costs $800 a month and I helped all the guys get cars with no car payments, well, okay, I bought them all a car, so Nick could stretch that $15 an hour pretty well."

"You bought all the guys a car?"

"Yeah," Damien said with a shrug. "Listen, none of them were going to get anywhere without a car. They weren't expensive cars – they were all used Corollas, about 10 years old, but very dependable. It wasn't that big a deal."

"Still, that's really nice of you," I said.

"Whatever. I don't want to focus on that. I need to figure out in my head what happened." He looked up at the ceiling. "Now I know why my fingerprints were on that lamp. I was meeting my father, and he intimidated me."

I was surprised by that. I didn't think *anybody* could intimidate Damien. Then again, Josh was an imposing figure. He was 6'4" and large-framed, like Lyndon Johnson. He spoke with a slight twang and was known for cussing people out over the slightest missteps. I understood Josh was responsible for many misdeeds but these misdeeds were only whispers. His handler, Tasha Bennington, was charged with cleaning up everything he ever did wrong and keeping it all out of the media. Josh had never received bad press but it was always common knowledge, in certain circles, that Josh really wasn't the saint he was made out to be.

Exhibit A on that was Olivia, Damien's mother. Olivia was raped by Josh when she was only 15. There had to be other Olivias out there. I also heard rumors and innuendo that multiple women were awarded hush-hush settlements due to Josh sexually harassing them. There were also stories about how shady a businessman Josh was – he would refuse to pay contractors what he owed them and then threatened them all with a lawsuit if they complained. Other stories I heard were that Josh was involved in insider trading. He had stock tips he acted on long before these tips became public knowledge.

The guy was a walking disaster but Tasha Bennington did her job very well. The media never picked up on any of it and neither did the authorities.

"He intimidated you?" I asked Damien. "In what way?"

Damien sighed. "I don't know. It's weird. I grew up with no father whatsoever, except for the men who would come through my mother's revolving door. Steven Harrington, who married my mother when she was 25, was the only guy who was even around for longer than a month and he beat the shit out of me on a regular basis. He was the reason I ran away and ended up on the streets and eventually in Ozanam. Now, suddenly, I have an actual father. And I know my actual father raped my mother and that was how I was conceived. Intellectually, I knew all that. But emotionally..." He shook his head. "It's weird, Harper, but I found myself wanting to please that guy. I don't really understand it myself, but whenever I met with him, I got nervous. I didn't want to say or do the wrong thing because I was..." He paused. "I was afraid he would reject me. There, I said it. I was afraid my rapist father would reject me."

In spite of myself, I smiled. Damien looked a bit like a young boy right at that moment. "That's nothing to be ashamed of. You haven't had a father your whole life, and, suddenly, you have a father. He might have been a bastard of a guy but he provided your DNA. I'm not surprised you felt that way about him."

"Yeah, well, it's embarrassing for me to admit to. But he made me feel like a bad kid in line to see the principal. He wasn't a warm man, to say the least. He was cold, aloof, inscrutable. I would sit his office, trying to get to know him, but getting words out of him was like pulling teeth. When I'm nervous like that, I tend to fidget. I pick up paper weights, touch things in my reach, my knee starts to shake up and down. I'm one of those guys who make other people nervous when I get nervous, which, thank God, isn't often. I don't usually get nervous about anything. But this guy made me nervous as hell."

"So, you were in his office," I said. "Why were you in his office in the first place?"

"That's where we always met. He was too busy to have a drink, go out to dinner or come over here for a meal. Whenever I wanted to talk to him, I had to do it in his office in between phone calls. That was the third time I met with him. He just got that lamp that day. His secretary gave it to him. Not sure exactly why the secretary got it for him, but that's what he said."

"He mentioned to you that the lamp was brand-new?"

"Yes, he mentioned that."

I wonder why he mentioned that. "Why did he tell you about the lamp?"

"I don't know, Harper." He hung his head and stared at his clasped hands. "We talked about things like that. It was so hard to get anything out of him, so I found myself desperately talking about anything I could think of. How the weather was that day, what he ate for lunch, is that a new lamp. It was a weird thing, Harper. I'm telling you, he unnerved me."

I still was having a hard time seeing Damien in that role – the role of the scared son who would do anything to please his cold and controlling father. He was always so confident, so assured. This was such a different tone for him. Such a different look. I didn't quite know how to approach this whole case.

"So you asking him about the lamp was just part of your

conversation with him? Because you couldn't really talk to him about anything else?"

"Yeah. I'm sure you've been in that situation. Everybody has, I think. You know, you're trying to talk to somebody and you just don't have anything to say to that person. And silence is really unnerving. So, you start babbling. That was me and Josh."

"Okay, well, I'm sure I can figure this out," I said. "At least I hope I can. First things first, though. I need to speak with Tasha Bennington. I'll bet she can give me some decent information. Not that she'll want to speak with me, but if I threaten her with a subpoena, she probably will talk. She literally knows where all the bodies are buried with this guy. Since her official position was Josh's fixer, I'm sure she'll be very valuable to my investigation."

"Yeah," Damien said. "And talk to Nick." He started to wring his hands. "If there's something in the air, somebody wanting to get revenge on me for the things I've done, it'll probably reach all the guys sooner or later. They have to keep their noses clean. They're all out on parole except Connor. He's completely free because his sentence was commuted down to 17 years. All the other guys had several more years to serve on their sentences when they were paroled. But Connor, who has a murder on his record, can ill afford to catch a case either." He sighed. "Harper, we're all in trouble. All of us. We have to figure this out."

I put my hand on Damien's shoulder. "Don't worry. I got this. But I just can't imagine somebody framing you by killing Josh Roland. Are you thinking the same person who allegedly framed you would've also framed Nick for embezzlement?" I shook my head. "I don't know. I still think the person who killed Josh had it in for him not necessarily you. After all, how would anybody know you touched that lamp? You were only in the office one time when that lamp was also in the office, right?"

"Yeah, but, come on Harper, it's a pretty safe bet I touched that lamp. It was within reach. I think the person who killed my father came in, had on rubber glove or used a cloth, picked up that lamp and killed my father with it, knowing I was in there and my fingerprints were probably on it. They also had to know that, since the lamp was brand-new, my fingerprints would be the only ones on it except my father's. I think person who did this had it in for me but also had it in for my father." He shook his head. "You have to start with that. The cross-section of whoever hated both my father and me."

"Governor Weston doesn't seem like the likeliest culprit at the moment. After all, Josh was very generous to Governor Weston. He was always feeding his campaign coffers to get favorable legislation for his businesses. That gravy train wasn't ending anytime soon. As long as Governor Weston was in Josh's pocket and benefiting from his largesse, I just don't see him killing that golden goose."

"Just keep it in mind," Damien said. "Please."

"Okay, okay, I will. But I'll start with Tasha. In the meantime, how are you holding up?"

Damien shrugged. "I don't really know. I'm still in shock." He sighed. "It's hard, Harper. It's hard to find out you have a father, even if that father is a cold bastard, and then, poof! Father is gone. Just like that. Before I even got a chance to know him."

I smiled. "That must be difficult. I must say, I got lucky, I guess. My father is now married to another man but I have an okay relationship with him. My mom is a pain in the ass, always picking at me, like mothers do, but we definitely love one another. I'm pretty close with my sisters and brothers, too, especially my younger sister Albany. We fight all the time as Irish people tend to do, but I have Sunday dinners with them and we always have each other's backs."

Damien looked wistful. "I wish I had that in my life. I really do. I'm becoming closer to my mom ever since I found out about what happened to her with my father raping her when she was only 15. She's a proud woman for all her faults. She won't accept my help for anything, especially monetary help. But I've tried to visit her once a month at her home. I suppose she's my family. Really, though, the guys are my family. I've never really had anybody else in my life, except my kids. I would do anything to have what you have with your parents and siblings."

He laughed lightly. "I actually thought I would have a relationship with my father. I don't know why I thought that. I guess because he showed some interest in seeing me. Even if I couldn't carry on a conversation with him, I figured that as long as I showed up, things could evolve eventually. Now..." He shook his head. "It's neither here nor there now, Harper. He's dead and there's nothing that can be done now."

I looked at the clock. "Well, it's 7. I really should be getting home to the girls. Will you be okay?"

Damien shrugged. "I guess." He grimaced. "My life is a mess right now, what can I say. My son hates me because he blames me for divorcing his mother. My daughter is in remission for a serious cancer that almost killed her and I live in fear it will come back. I'm being accused of murder. Realistically, it's not looking too good for me. I have motive, means and opportunity to have killed him. I guess things could be worse. I could be living in Ukraine or some other war-torn country, but things seem pretty bleak right now."

I didn't want to leave Damien. I knew he really didn't have anybody he could confide in. He had the guys, but, because he was out on bail, he couldn't associate with any of them as they were all convicted felons. That was one of the conditions of his bail – he couldn't associate with convicted felons except on a professional basis. He had his kids, but, if he was like most parents, he would want to shield them from the reality of his situation. He wouldn't want to scare them. He had to lean on me and I would give him my all.

Yet, I had to get home to the girls. I had to put them first.

"Will you be okay?" I asked again.

Damien hung his head. I had never seen him look so defeated. So lost. "Yeah, Harper, I'll be fine. Get home to your girls. Don't worry about me."

I nodded. "I'll see you in the office?"

"Yeah. I'll be coming into work every day. That'll be my only source of sanity."

I put my hand on his shoulder. "Okay. I'll see you tomorrow."

"Tomorrow."

I left Damien's house with a heavy heart. He wasn't himself. He was accessing a part of him he had tried to hide from the world. The shadow part of him wounded by life. I knew that when I looked at him in his house. It worried me.

I didn't think Damien would hurt himself when he got like this.

But maybe I didn't know him as well as I thought.

CHAPTER 5

I got home and Rina and Abby demanded to know what was going on. "I heard Damien is in trouble," Rina said. "Everybody's talking about it in school. I heard he killed his father. Tell me that's not true, Mom."

"Oh, Rina," I said. "Who did you hear that from?"

"I go to school with Josh Roland's granddaughter, Hannah, or did you forget that? She talked to me about it. She knows Damien is your law partner, too, and she's been rubbing it in my face that you're associated with a murderer."

I groaned. I *did* forget that one of Rina's classmates was Josh's granddaughter but I should've remembered that. After all, Rina and Abby went to one of the most, if not the most, exclusive prep schools in Kansas City. It stood to reason they would have classmates kin to Josh Roland.

"What did Hannah tell you?" I was interested to find out what Josh's granddaughter knew about the situation. Maybe I could glean some clues from what she knew. Everything helped.

"She said Damien was Josh's son and had reason to kill Josh.

Something about him wanting to cover something up about his friend, Nick. But Mom, that doesn't really make so much sense, does it?"

"What do you mean?"

"Well, I guess Nick was stealing from the company but anybody would know that. The evidence was right there. I heard Nick was about to be arrested for stealing. Why would Damien kill Josh if there was still evidence Nick was stealing? It didn't seem to do any good, did it? Killing Josh?"

I shook my head. My young daughter was so intelligent it was scary. She had such a logical brain. Abby did too, but Abby didn't always try to argue with me as much as Rina did. Rina was always springing creative arguments on me to get out of things, which was how I knew how much Rina used her logical thinking skills.

"No, you're right about that one, Lady Bug. No indeed."

"But Hannah also said there was another reason why Damien might have killed his dad."

"Oh? What is that reason?"

"Something about how Damien was pushed into it by his mother. I don't really understand it, though, Mom."

"Well, that makes little sense to me, either." I didn't imagine Damien would kill for his mother. I knew everybody had it in them to commit murder under the right circumstances. That was a truism. But, thus far, I hadn't seen any kind of circumstance that would compel Damien to kill his father. And Rina was right – Nick's alleged crime was something easily proved by a paper trail. Killing Josh wouldn't have covered up that alleged crime.

"Did Hannah tell you anything else?" I asked Rina. "About her grandfather's murder?"

"No," Rina said, shaking her head. "She hates me now, though. And Abby. Not that I care. I never liked her anyway.

She's kind of rude and mean so it's no biggie if she doesn't like me and Abby anymore." She brushed her shoulder. "I just let it roll right off my back, Mom."

I looked over at Abby. "What about you? Did Hannah talk to you about this?"

Abby shrugged. "No, Mom. She never did talk to me much. She's in a different group than me."

That was true. Abby hung out with the bookworms and gamer geeks. Rina was part of the popular group. I figured Hannah was also part of that clique but it seemed Rina didn't really care if Hannah hated her so maybe Hannah didn't have that much influence.

Just then, I heard my doorbell ring. "I wonder who that is?" I said aloud. I wasn't expecting anybody.

I was always cautious, especially since that day when I came home and found Officer Cooper waiting for me to come home. He intimated he would harm my girls and that freaked me out to no end. It was almost 8 PM and it was quite dark outside.

I looked through my peephole and saw Nick Savante standing right outside my door. "Oh, it's just Nick," I said. "I'm sure he wants to talk about his case."

Abby and Rina both rolled their eyes. "Mom, we haven't eaten yet," Abby said. "Can't you tell him to go away and come back later?"

"I could but that would be rude," I said.

"Isn't it rude for him just to show up like this?"

"I guess, but, girls, you'll just have to live with it, won't you? Now go and set another place for Nick to have dinner with us."

More rolling of the eyes, but Abby begrudgingly went into the kitchen with Rina and they were soon putting plates and silverware on the table.

I opened the door. "Hey, Nick," I said. "Come on in."

"Thanks, Harper," Nick said. He looked embarrassed. "I'm sorry to be bothering you like this but I was in the neighborhood. I actually tried to see Damien but he turned me away. Said he has a cop living across the street from him and if that cop saw me in his house, he would be violating his bail and would have to spend his pre-trial period in jail. I don't want to do that to him, so..." He shook his head. "Then I saw your house and thought I would take a chance."

"Well, I'm glad you did. We're about to have dinner. Won't you join us?"

Nick looked embarrassed again. "Oh, I'm so sorry. I guess I thought you probably already ate."

"Yes," I said, "we eat late a lot of times because I work late so much. But I've made plenty. Beef Stroganoff."

"I can come back," he said. "Later."

"I won't hear of it." I put my arm around his shoulder. "Mi casa su casa."

He finally nodded his head. "I actually love beef stroganoff," he said. "Let me help you set the table or something."

"The girls are doing just that," I said. "It's all under control."

"Well, thanks," he said. He went into the dining room where the table was set and there was a tureen in the middle filled to the brim with stroganoff and noodles. "Looks delicious."

"I like to think I'm a decent cook," I said. "Sit down, let me pour you a glass of wine." I didn't drink myself but I was at the point where I could have wine in the house for guests and not be tempted to down it. My new AA sponsor, Haley Lightner, was helping with that. I found myself calling her frequently and she was always able to talk me off the ledge.

I got the wine out, poured him a glass and he took a sip. "Delicious," he said.

Over dinner, I noticed Nick ate his food eagerly. I wondered if he was eating enough at his home. I had a feeling he wasn't. He was living with Tommy Arcola, Damien told me, in a small two-bedroom apartment on the East Side. They both were fresh out of prison so I doubted either guy knew much about cooking. This guy probably lived off fast food. At any rate, it seemed he hadn't been treated to a home-cooked meal in awhile by the looks of things.

"This is the best I've ever eaten," Nick said. "Seriously."

"Well, it's really not hard to make. I slow-cook the meat in a crock pot and then just add broth, sour cream and mushrooms to it. I try to have something green on the plate, too, so I usually make asparagus spears or artichoke hearts. The girls like those vegetables." I served this particular dinner with a side of asparagus spears I steamed and put butter on. "It's really a snap. You should learn how to make simple dishes like this one. What are you eating at your house?"

He shrugged. "Frozen pizza, fast food, that type of thing. I'm not a gourmet cook and neither is Tommy. We're lucky if we get a rotisserie chicken once a week."

I smiled. "You and Tommy should come over more often," I said. "And maybe I can show you a few things around the kitchen."

"That would be great," Nick said. "I'm eager to learn, really. I mean, I've spent 17 years being fed three times a day. It was crap food but it was food. Now I have to fend for myself and it's hard to do."

"Well, come on over a few times a month and I'll feed you guys. You just have to help me cook."

"Will do." Nick smiled and then looked shyly at the two girls. I took that to mean he needed to speak with me alone.

"Abby, Rina," I said to the girls. "Go upstairs to your rooms and get your homework done. When you're done, you can do whatever you want." Abby liked to play chess on-line and was getting quite good at it, from what I could tell. Rina, for her part, usually got on Facebook or chatted with her friends online. Sometimes the girls would watch something on Netflix or HBO. Abby was also getting interested in video games and Rina told me Abby was becoming a gamer geek, whatever that meant.

They groaned but both went upstairs to their rooms.

"Sorry," Nick said, looking ashamed. "I shouldn't have intruded on your family."

"Nick, it's not a problem, honest. You came to me because I think you need to talk to me. I'm all ears. But I must warn you, I can't represent you. As it's looking now, I believe your criminal case is a conflict of interest with Damien because the cops think Damien killed his father to protect you."

"I know and that's ridiculous if you want to know the truth. This whole thing is ridiculous. I didn't steal from Josh. I'm not trying to go back to the joint, Harper. I certainly wouldn't mess things up by doing something like that. I make enough money to get by. I really do. I have another three years left on my parole. I wouldn't catch a case like that."

"I know," I said. "But who would frame you like that? I just don't understand any of it."

"I don't know but it seems convenient. I get framed and then so does Damien. Apparently I was framed to make it seem Damien killed his father just to protect me, but, here I am, being questioned for stealing from Josh. It seems Damien didn't do a very good job of protecting me if that's what they're saying."

I nodded. "You've been questioned but not arrested?"

"Right. They didn't arrest me for anything."

I raised my eyebrow. That didn't seem right to me. Why didn't they just arrest him? If they had the goods on him wouldn't they slap him with an arrest warrant and send him to his parole officer for a violation? What were they waiting for?

"Have you seen an attorney about this yet?"

"No. I can't afford one. If they arrest me and throw me in jail, I can get a Public Defender, but, at the moment, nothing has happened. I don't qualify for any kind of court-appointed attorney just yet."

"That's true, you don't," I said. "I wish I could advise you, but..."

"I know. I guess I just have to wait and see if the cops come back and arrest me. I hate doing that, Harper, but it is what it is. In the meantime, I have to find another job. I might end up working construction with Jack. It's wintertime, or it almost is, so those jobs will be scarce. It's rough out there for us ex-cons."

"Damien is afraid all of you guys will end up getting arrested for something," I said. "What do you think about that?"

"I think you might be right, although I don't know why I believe that. Why does Damien believe that?"

"I think because Damien told me what happened with the governor. He thinks the governor is out to get him."

Nick shook his head and looked at me. "I don't know what you're talking about Harper," he said. "What are you talking about, the governor's out to get him?"

"He didn't tell you?"

"No, he didn't tell me."

I studied his face and realized he was telling the truth. He didn't know what Damien had done with the governor. He didn't know about the blackmail. He didn't know about any of that.

"Nick, Damien did something with the governor. He had some information on him - something that would sink him. He used this information against him to get Connor's sentence commuted. I'm surprised he didn't tell you about that."

Nick looked very confused."I guess it makes sense. None of us could figure out how Connor got out of prison with the rest of us. And I know the governor has caught a lot of flack for doing that for him. I guess it makes sense that blackmail was involved. I know Damien would do anything to make sure we got out of prison. And that includes Connor."

"So yeah, Damien now thinks the governor is out to get him. He thinks the blackmail was behind his arrest for killing Josh Roland and your arrest for stealing from Josh. And I wonder why they questioned you and didn't charge. That makes me think some kind of a game is being played. Like maybe they know the charges against you won't stick which is why won't charge you. However, if they claim you were under suspicion for stealing from Josh Roland, then it makes sense -it would give Damien motive for killing Josh."

"I guess I don't really understand. What are you trying to say, Harper?"

"I don't really know. It's just something I'm speculating about. I have a feeling you will never be charged for stealing from Josh. I have a feeling they have no actual evidence you did something like that. I think they only accused you of stealing to give Damien a motive for having killed Josh."

Nick looked contemplative when I said that. "Okay, I guess it makes sense." But he looked skeptical. "Who would do something like that? Somebody went through an awful lot of trouble."

"Somebody who wanted to kill Josh and frame Damien. It's pretty simple if you think about it."

Nick shook his head. "I knew a lot of guys in prison but somehow I'm skeptical about something so devious. And so well planned out."

"Trust me, I've been doing this for so long that nothing surprises me anymore."

Nick patted his legs, a sure sign he was getting ready to leave. "Well, Harper," he said. "Thanks a lot for letting me come here and talk to you about this. I was hoping maybe you could do something for me but I understand you can't because you're representing Damien and obviously my case is intertwined with his. Let me know if there's anything I can do to help you with your case for Damien."

"I will. Thanks for that."

I watched him walk off and the girls came downstairs. "What did Nick want?" Rina asked.

"Nothing, Lady Bug," I said. "He just wanted to speak with me about something. It's not your business."

"Oh really? What about what Hannah said about Nick stealing from Josh?"

"Rina, I won't talk to you about this," I said. "Now it's time for you to go to bed."

Rina groaned a little but eventually went up to her room. Abby, for her part, was standing back with her arms crossed in front of her.

"Buttercup," I said, "what's going on?"

"Nothing Mom," Abby said, her head hanging down.

"There's something going on. I can tell."

"No Mom," Abby said. "There's nothing going on."

I knew she was lying. There was something bothering her. I decided not to press.

"Okay Abby," I said. "It's getting late so you need to go to bed."

Abby shook her head and went upstairs.

I wondered how much time I had before Abby started to give me a lot of trouble.

It was always the quiet ones.

CHAPTER 6

The next day I went to see Tasha Bennington. Her office was in one of the downtown high-rises on one of the top floors. Her official job was public relations, but almost everyone knew her version of public relations meant she fixed things for wealthy people. If there was a CEO accused of sexual harassment or a billionaire's son was raping women, she kept him out of the news. She had a lot of friends at the newspaper and many media contacts. She called on favors when she needed to and was not above blackmailing and bribing people to make sure secrets stayed buried.

She was expecting me so I didn't have to wait long to see her. I waited in her suite for five minutes before she came out and shook my hand.

"Hello Ms. Ross," she said. "I understand you're here to speak with me about Josh Roland."

"Yes. As you know, my client, Damian Harrington, has been accused of murdering him. I need to talk to you about what you know about people who might have had motive to kill him."

"I'll do whatever I can to help," she said. "However, you understand that just because my client is dead doesn't mean I want his secrets getting out. You'll need to sign a nondisclosure agreement. I hope you don't mind."

"How will that work? I'll have to subpoena your witnesses to show up to court so I can show Josh Roland had a lot of enemies. Your nondisclosure agreement would prevent me from doing that."

"Those are my terms," she said.

"Those terms are unacceptable," I said.

"You have to understand, Ms. Ross," she said. "If I start telling secrets about my clients, my business will go belly up. Nobody wants their secrets coming out after they're dead. What I get paid a lot of money to do is ensure my clients don't have their reputations besmirched in the media."

"Oh, I understand. But you have to understand me. I'm defending Damien Harrington for murder. If I have to, I'll subpoena you. I'll put you under oath and ask you questions. Either way, you'll give me the information I seek."

"I'll quash your subpoena on the grounds that your questioning me will be a fishing expedition."

"You can try to quash the subpoena all you want," I said. "It won't work. It's pretty obvious that whatever you tell me will be something relevant to the case. I have to show the jury alternative suspects. I think you know this. I'm sure you've been called to testify in court before."

"I've not been involved with anybody murdering one of my clients yet. I suppose there's a first time for everything."

"You mean to tell me you've never been involved in a court case before? I find that hard to believe. Even if you've not been involved in someone murdering one of your clients, I'm quite sure somebody has sued for things your clients have done. I understand your whole job is ensuring charges are never brought against your clients. I understand you're friendly with most of the police department and have dirt on just about everybody in law enforcement. The ones you cannot blackmail, I know you bribe. I understand all that. That said, if you're involved in a civil lawsuit, there's no getting around a subpoena. So I'd like to know how you've managed to stay out of court."

She studied me, her cool green eyes focused on my face. She tapped one of her fingers on her cheeks as she stared at me and smiled a little bit. "Let's just say I have somebody in my pocket who ensures I don't have to testify in court for anything. Believe me, you are vulnerable in this. Anybody who ever tried to get me to testify in court ended up in court themselves. I know what happened with Damien. I know about him suborning perjury, and I know about him blackmailing the governor. I have those two things working in my favor."

I had no idea how she managed to get that information, but knew she was dangerous. Anybody who had this kind of information about Damien was dangerous. I wondered if she had some information about me. I didn't know. I knew, however, that she could definitely get Damien disbarred if she wanted to.

"I also know things about you," she said. "I think you better be careful."

"What kinds of things do you know about me?"

"I know you have enough cocaine in your car right now that if I called the police with an anonymous tip, you'd be arrested and thrown in jail. I would make sure the charges stick."

I shook my head. "Is that all you have? I think you know I don't have any cocaine in my car right now."

"And you think I don't have ways of planting drugs in your car? Are you really that naïve?" It was her turn to shake her head. "You don't think I have somebody who could get a search warrant for your car who will plant whatever he wants and have you arrested? Look what happened to your client Darnell

Williams. Look what happened to him. Do you see how easy it is to get someone in trouble when they've done nothing wrong?"

I suddenly understood exactly why she was so good at her job. She was ruthless and would do anything. I narrowed my eyes. I also thought about I got stopped all those years ago and marijuana was supposedly found in my car. That pot was put there by a cop. A cop trying to intimidate me. Now here was this woman trying to do the exact same thing.

"I'm going to find out about what Josh did, whether you tell me or not."

"I understand that. That's not what I'm trying to intimidate you about. What I'm trying to say is that nothing Josh has done will come from me. And if you try to subpoena me for trial to speak about what I know about my client Josh, I will ruin you. I have the means to do it. I've dealt with lesser people than you before. She crossed her arms in front of her and narrowed her green eyes at me again. "And I can probably make your policeman boyfriend dance for me. I could use it against you. I know things about him you don't know, things that could send him to prison for a very long time. I have that in my back pocket."

"What are you talking about?" She knew things about Axel I didn't know? Was she just trying to intimidate me? She'd been trying to intimidate me this entire time, so I imagined that was all it was. She didn't really know anything about Axel.

She smiled. "Now you're wondering, aren't you? You're wondering what I know about your boyfriend? I understand. You're looking at me and thinking I'm just blowing smoke up your ass. But you don't really know, though, do you? You think maybe it's true. You think maybe he did something illegal. After all, he's a cop. Cops are always involved in all kinds of dirty things. What makes you think your boyfriend is so clean?"

"Okay, I'll call your bluff. You tell me what my boyfriend has done."

She rolled her eyes. "You think I'm just going to tell you? No, I'm not going tell you anything. You'll have to find out for yourself if you subpoena me for court."

I wouldn't play her game. "Well, then, I don't think he did anything wrong. If he did something wrong, tell me what it is."

"You don't know how I work. Obviously. I don't want to implicate other people on the force, so I will only pull out what I know about your boyfriend if I have to. Which means if I get a subpoena for court, Axel will be in trouble with the force, probably will be go to prison, and so will you. I understand you're clean. But you have to know how easy it is to plant something so you're not so clean."

I sighed. I was defeated. If I would find out anything about Josh Roland, it wouldn't come from this woman. I would have to do my detective work. It wouldn't be as easy as the fixer telling me what I wanted to know about Josh Roland and hope she would tell me everything she knew. I should have known she was sworn to confidentiality and it was her business to ensure sure all high-level people got away with their crimes. I was nothing special. I was just another person for her to black-mail into doing what she wanted.

"I see you're not going to help me. And I can't subpoena you. But know this—I will find out what Josh was up to. And I will find out who had it in for him."

"That's fine," she said, "as long as it doesn't come from me, that's fine. Now I'll show you out and would recommend you don't ever come here again. And if I get a subpoena in the mail, excuse me, if I get a subpoena served to me by one of your process servers, the next thing that'll happen is that both you and Axel will be in prison and Damien will be disbarred. Fair warning."

As I walked out of her office, I wondered if the governor also had this woman on his side. If that was the case, Damien was probably right when he said he was set up. This woman played hardball like nobody I'd ever seen.

I had to admire her just a little bit .

I called Damien the next day and told him what happened with Tasha Bennington.

"Dammit, Damien, it'll be harder than I thought to find out what your father was up to. I spoke with his fixer, Tasha Bennington, and she was no help at all. In fact, she said that if I try to subpoena her you'll be disbarred for what you did with Gina, go to prison for what you did to the governor, and would also make sure Axel got into trouble, because apparently he's up to no good. I think. I hope that isn't right and she was making up lies to ensure I did what she wanted. Then again, I wouldn't put anything past anybody, even Axel. I've been in this business long enough to know that nobody is above anything. Guess I'm cynical."

Damien looked at me funny, but I could tell he was in agreement.

It was true you really never know the person you love. It was entirely possible Axel lived a double life. I knew that. I wanted to trust him. I wanted to trust everybody in my life. But it was impossible to do so. When you worked in the field I worked in and saw so many people who committed heinous crimes behind their lover's back, you get a bit jaded.

"What is it that Axel was supposedly doing?" Damien asked.

"It's not necessarily relevant to your case, so I don't want to talk about that so much until I know what the hell is going on. What's relevant is that Tasha Bennington won't be any help in your case and won't testify in court. I would like to subpoena her for court, of course, because I think she knows where all the bodies are buried. Probably literally. However, she's threatening you, Axel and me, and I won't go there. So we need to talk to Tom Garrett and see if he can find out information about your father."

"That's good thinking. It has to be all hands on deck for this. We're up against a powerful, well-protected enemy. And from what you tell me, we're not only up against Josh but also up against the governor."

"That's very true," I said, "we have to look at that angle for sure."

Then he sighed.

"Damien," I said. "I get the feeling you've been very depressed and down. I don't blame you, of course. You lost your father. Even though you didn't really know him, I know you had high hopes for having an relationship with him. And now you're accused of murdering him. Are there any other problems you're having right now? I just need to know."

Damien shook his head. "My ex-wife Sarah is back in the picture. She's been acting erratically. She's been calling my daughter Amelia, crying on the phone, asking Amelia to forgive her. And then she calls back, after Amelia told her she doesn't want to talk to her, and starts cursing at her. I wish there was something legally I could do to make her stop calling my daughter. I looked into getting a restraining order against her. All I've been told is that what she's been doing doesn't rise to the level of harassment."

"What kinds of things does she say to your daughter?"

"She's been telling lies. Amelia has asked me if I'm really her father. Sarah apparently told Amelia I'm not really her father but somebody else is."

"Is that possible?"

"As you say about Axel, anything is possible. I don't really know. Sarah cheated on me when Amelia was sick and eventually moved in with the guy with whom she was cheating. That much I can tell you. So Sara was definitely capable of cheating. And it's true that Amelia doesn't really look like me. Nate certainly does. So I don't really know the answer to that question, but whatever the answer is, Amelia is my daughter no matter what. Even if she does not share my DNA, she's my daughter."

"Sarah hasn't threatened her, has she?"

"I don't think so, but if she threatened me with taking her away, what could she do?"

"I don't do family law cases. I've only done criminal cases. But, from what little I know, I think it's a matter of her filing a paternity petition and making you take a paternity test. However, even if it's proven in court that Amelia is not biologically your child, it's entirely possible the judge won't do anything to sever your parental rights. The judge has to look at the best interest of the child. The best interest of the child in this case is clearly for Amelia to stay with you. So I wouldn't worry about that too much."

Damien nodded. "I guess I wouldn't worry about it legally, but Amelia has been through so much with her illness. And now she thinks I'm not really her father. This whole thing just makes me want to vomit."

I put my hand on his shoulder and squeezed hard. "You're going through a lot. I understand that. I'm here for you, not just legally, but as a friend of course."

Damien nodded. "I just don't know what Sarah is capable of. I didn't tell you this, but she attempted suicide when the two of us were broken up. She was in the mental hospital for a week or maybe even longer, which is what typically happens when you attempt suicide. I know she has some mental issues. I don't really know what they are, however I know she has them. So I'm really afraid she'll come after my daughter."

"Has she made any threats against you?"

"No. That's a good thing, of course."

"Has she made threats against Nate?"

"No. Nate hates me for leaving her and would like to speak with his mother. So now, even though Sarah's threatening Amelia, Nate's jealous, if you can believe that. He's jealous Amelia is talking to Sarah and he isn't."

"Oh, I can believe that."

"Anyhow," Damien said, "that's what's going on with me. I'm very upset, of course, about being under investigation for murder, but I'm not even that upset about the possibility that I might go to prison, because I've been there before. I know I can last. I'm more upset about the possibility I'll lose my kids. I know you have guardianship of them if something ever happened to me. However, I worry that if Sara can prove I'm not Amelia's father, if I went to prison, then Amelia would would end up with Sarah. And since I don't know if Sarah is mentally stable, I think that's dangerous."

I didn't really know what to say to Damien about all this. I knew he was probably right. If he went to prison, then Sarah would probably get custody of at least Amelia, even though Damien legally gave me guardianship over both kids. It was a touchy situation anyway, because even though Damien gave me guardianship, Damien never got Sarah's permission for me to have the guardianship. Sarah could challenge it, no matter what. And I could see Damien was afraid of that happening.

"Damien, I wish I had something good to say to you, but I just don't at the moment. But don't worry. This investigation is just beginning. I haven't spoken with any of the people I plan on deposing as witnesses, so I don't really know what direction this will go. What I know is I'll turn over every single stone on this because your life is at stake."

"Is it literally at stake? Have they decided to seek the death penalty?"

"No, they haven't certified your case yet for the death penalty. However, I've been in touch with the prosecuting attorney on this case. It's Nick Wright. He told me they're considering it."

Damien chuckled. "I guess this is cause for gallows humor right about now, huh? Man, here I am, a criminal defense attorney, and I might end up death row. This is a made-for-Netflix documentary if ever there was one."

"Damien, please don't worry about that. I swear to God I'll get you out of this. If it's the last thing I do."

"This just might be the last thing you do."

I looked to him knowing there was a possibility he just might be right about that.

This might be the last thing I did.

CHAPTER 7

When I got into the car, I decided to meet with Tom Garrett and see what he could find out more about Damien's background. But I first would have to deal with Axel, who was calling me on the phone in my car.

"Hey, lass," Axel said. "What do you say to me coming over tonight and bringing a movie and pizza for your kids? We can have a movie night at your house."

"That sounds like fun, Axel," I said. "However, I need to talk to you about something."

"What do you want talk to me about?"

"I just came from Tasha Bennington's office. I wanted to subpoena her for court because I needed to find out information about who had it in for Josh Roland. She knows where the bodies are buried as far as that goes. From what I understand, Josh Roland has been in a lot of trouble over the years. I don't know what kinds of trouble. I know he raped Damien's mother. I've heard he's been on the wrong end of sexual harassment claims. I've heard rumors about all kinds of illegal things. I don't know what else he has done - there might be plenty of other wrongful acts committed and I need to find out what they are. However, Tasha has threatened me by telling me that if I tried to subpoena her for court she'll plant drugs on me and have me arrested."

"Well I wouldn't mess with her too much, mate," Axel said. "Don't worry, I'm sure you can find out plenty about Josh Roland without talking to her."

"I know I can. However, there's something she said to me that disturbed me. Something about you."

"And what is that, mate?"

"She said you've been involved in illegal things on the police department. That you're essentially a dirty cop. I don't believe that about you, of course. I think she is just blowing smoke up my ass and trying to create things out of whole cloth. However, I wanted to talk to you about it and get your side of the story."

Axel became very quiet.

"Axel? Are you still there?"

"Mate, let's talk about this later."

My heart started to race. I started having trouble breathing. "Axel, that's not the reaction I expected from you."

"What kind of reaction did you expect from me? You're asking me these things and it's clear you don't trust me."

"Should I trust you?"

"You know me very well, mate. No, I'm not involved with anything illegal. There's much more to this story. I don't really want to talk about it over the phone. Let me come over tonight and we'll talk about it when I see you."

I didn't like that reaction either. "You sound like someone I need to be concerned about, to say the very least." I took a deep breath. "Okay Axel, come on over 7 o'clock tonight. We'll have pizza and watch a movie and you and I can talk about whatever's going on."

"Okay, mate," Axel said. "I'll see you then."

I hung up and suddenly was focused on what was going on with Axel. I knew I couldn't focus that much on him, however, because I had Damien's case to worry about. Damien's case would be difficult to win. I had a feeling Tasha Bennington was so good at covering up what Josh had done that it would be a tough road trying to figure out the illegal and wrong things Josh had been up to.

Now I would also have to worry about Axel.

I sighed as I went to meet Tom Garrett at one of his favorite bars downtown. My mind was certainly not on the task at hand, because I was so concerned about what Axel would tell me that night.

I got into the bar and saw Tom. He stood up and smiled. "How's it going Harper?" Tom asked me.

"Okay, I guess. How are you?"

"Can't complain."

"Well I'm coming to see you, of course, because I'm Damien's attorney and Damien is restricted in his movements at the moment. He had to either stay at home or go to and from work. But you should really go see him. He can't get visits from his friends Nick, Connor, Jack and Tommy. They're all convicted felons and he's restricted from seeing them. I think he's getting kind of lonely over there. He's having a lot of issues with his ex-wife Sarah too."

"That's hard to hear," Tom said, "however, I'm also a convicted felon. I guess you forgot that."

That was true - I *did* forget that he was also a convicted felon.

"Ok. Guess you can't see him either. That's too bad."

Tom looked amused and embarrassed at the same time. "Well, what do you need me to do on Damien's case?"

"I need you to investigate Josh Roland. I specifically need to know who his enemies were. I tried to get information out of Tasha Bennington, but suffice to say it did not go well."

"Tasha Bennington?" Tom whistled under his breath and shook his head. "That woman is a piece of work. No, of course you won't get anything out of her. She knows better than that."

"That's true," I said. "She's a piece of work."

"What do you expect from a woman who makes her living covering up for the rich and famous?" Tom asked. "You understand she not only works for locals, but also works for people around the globe. If you ever wonder why wealthy people are rarely in the news for their misdeeds, it's because of people like Tasha Bennington."

I nodded. "So, as I said, since Tasha Bennington won't help me, I need all hands on deck. I need you to figure out where the bodies are buried when it comes to Josh Roland. I need for you to turn over every stone you can."

"Okay. That goes without saying."

"I know, but I'm saying it anyway."

Tom took a sip of his whiskey, and, as usual, I started to salivate. I so wanted some of his whiskey. "Where do you want me to begin?" he asked.

"Well, I'm talking to Damien's mom tomorrow. I don't know how that will go. What kind of relationship did Damien and his mother have?"

"It was strained for many years. Damien wasn't close with his mother because Olivia was never a good mother. She was too much into drink, drugs, and prostitution. However, once Damien found out his mother was raped and that was how he was conceived, he decided to forgive her. He didn't realize until he found out she was raped that there was a reason for her acting the way she did all these years."

"So Damien and his mother have a better relationship?" I felt for Damien and really felt for his mother. I certainly could relate to his mother's behavior. If she was taking drugs, she was no doubt trying to forget what happened to her. That was much of the reason why I started to drink heavily - I needed to forget what had happened to me.

"I guess so. However, that doesn't mean his mother would be above doing something like this. I know that's what you're thinking - maybe Olivia did this."

"That actually was what I was thinking, but what are you trying to say?"

"There's a possibility Damien's mother would've killed Josh Roland. And, I wouldn't put it past her to frame her son."

"Why would she kill Josh Roland?" I actually knew the answer to that question, but wanted Tom's take on it.

Tom took another sip of his whiskey and then looked like he was contemplating the question. "Harper, let me just tell you something I think is suspicious. Damien's mother went for years without telling Damien who his father is. She consistently told him his father was a rando at the club where she worked. And she was with a lot of different men. She told Damien she met up with some guy, they had sex, she got pregnant. However, she told Damien she didn't know which guy was his father because she was doing so many different guys. She never once told him the possibility that his father was a billionaire and a very prominent citizen in Kansas City."

"So what? So she kept it from him. What does that have to do with anything?" I asked. Tom was getting at something, but I wasn't quite following his train of thought.

"I'll tell you what I think is odd about that situation. She wanted Damien to know Josh after she kept Josh's paternity a secret from him all these years. She wanted to keep Josh a secret when Damien was younger because she didn't want Josh to take custody. She told Damien she thought that if he knew who his father was when he was younger, he would go and stay with him. And, according to Olivia, Damien's mother didn't want that to happen because she was afraid Damien would fall prey to his crazy family."

"What kind of crazy family does Josh have?"

"His sister Darla has been diagnosed with bipolar disorder and schizophrenia. She's been in and out of institutions for many years. She also has been on drugs. Josh's kids are both problems. I've heard stories that his son, John, has raped many women and might even have killed some women. I've also heard stories that his daughter, Katie, is involved in a doomsday cult. Olivia knew this about Josh's family. She knew they were involved with drugs and had a lot of mental illness going through their blood. She didn't want Damien to have anything to do with that. At least that's what she told Damien about why she didn't want him involved with Josh's family."

I was writing everything down as he spoke with me. I looked up at him. "Okay then, here's my next question. What does this have to do with anything? What does this have to do with your suspecting that Olivia might have been involved in Josh Roland's murder?"

"Well I thought it was very odd that Olivia, after keeping Damien's father's secret from him for all these years, chose to finally tell him who his father was. Not only that but she went to Josh and told him he had a child named Damien. And then lied about it."

"What do you mean she lied about it? What did she say to Damien?"

"At first, she told Damien the truth. She told him she went to Josh to tell him he had a son. And then she came out with another story and told Damien that Josh sought her out to speak with her out of the blue. She said Josh was in AA and trying to make amends for raping her all these years ago. You know something about AA and making amends, don't you Harper?"

"Oh yes, of course. That's one of the biggest things about Alcoholics Anonymous. You must make amends to the people you've hurt." I took a sip of my soda water and lime. "That's what Olivia told Damien about why Josh sought her out?"

"Yes, that's what Olivia told Damien."

I wrote this down "What are you thinking, Tom, about the real reason why Olivia sought out Josh after all these years and told Josh about Damien?"

"If you want to know the truth, I wouldn't put it past Olivia to do that for one reason only. She planned on killing Josh and framing her own son for it. Think about it. The only reason why Damien established a relationship with his father was because Olivia told Josh about Damien. Correct?"

"I suppose that's right."

"Of course it's right. Damien wanted nothing to do with his father until Olivia told Josh about him and Josh said he wanted to see him. I know that for a fact. Now, all of a sudden, Josh is calling Damien and Damien is going to see him. Olivia was the reason why any of that happened. Is any of this just a little bit suspicious?"

"Okay. So you're saying Olivia killed Josh and framed her own son."

"No, that's not what I'm saying. But it might've happened that way. I'm saying it's a possibility. Don't foreclose that possibility. That's all I'm saying."

I chewed on my pen as I thought about what he said. I didn't know. I had never met Olivia. I didn't know her from Eve. I supposed it was a possibility. Hell, if I thought Axel was involved with illegal activities, I could certainly think that about Olivia. If there was one thing I learned in my years of criminal defense it was that nobody was ever how they seemed. People can surprise the hell out of you.

"Okay then, what else do you know about this case? What else do you know about anybody who might have been out to get Josh?

"I know as much as you do as far as that goes, which is not much. However, I'll do my investigation and know I'll come up with a number of people who might've had a problem with the man. Don't worry, we'll figure this out in the end."

I took a deep breath. I didn't know if I should go there, but I felt I needed to. "I don't know if you know this, but..." Then I decided not to say anything to him about what Damien had done with the governor and Gina. Damien had not given me permission to say anything, therefore I didn't feel it was my place.

"But what?"

"Nothing."

I wasn't putting anything over on Tom. He seemed to know what I was thinking. "Listen, I know what happened with the governor. I was there. In fact, I helped Damien with that situation. Damien needed me to verify the person who sent the dick-pic to Jackson was the governor and I did that. So I know what he did with Governor Weston."

That surprised me, although it probably shouldn't have. I wondered if he knew about what happened with Damien and Gina. I doubted he did.

"Damien believes the governor might be behind all this because the governor wanted to get back at him. So that's something I need to follow up on. I have to figure out if the governor has some kind of issue with Josh. Doesn't make much sense to me right now but maybe it will in the future."

"It probably will," Tom said. "I wouldn't be surprised if it will. Anyhow, I think you might find some surprising things when you dig deep."

"Why do you say that?"

Tom shrugged. "I don't know. I've just heard things about the governor that make me think he might not be the moral and pious man he shows to the world. And I don't mean just because he happened to send a dick pic to a man. Okay?"

"What are you thinking?"

"What I'm thinking there's a possibility that Josh knew something about the governor and was about ready to reveal it. To shut him up, the governor decided to kill him and framed Damien because he hates Damien for causing him so many problems with the Connor commutation issue. Maybe two birds one stone. That's my take on the situation."

That was an interesting thought. Maybe it was true. Maybe the governor deduced something that Josh knew about or maybe there was some other reason why the governor would've killed Josh. It seemed kind of flimsy to me, but then again, I'd been surprised before in my investigations. Perhaps this was just the same kind of situation.

"What else do you know, Tom?" I asked him.

"I don't know right now, but I'll find out, that's for sure."

"Thanks." I bit my lower lip and shook my head. I would have ask him something else. Something that made me feel extremely uncomfortable to say the very least.

I'd have to ask the question anyway.

"What's on your mind, Harper?" Tom asked.

I took a deep breath and let it out slowly. "Well Tom," I began. "You know I'm dating somebody whose named is Axel right?"

"Of course, of course, Axel," Tom said. "Good guy."

"Yes. Great guy. However, when I went to talk to Bennington she told me Axel might've been involved in some illegal activities on the police force. He denies it, but he's coming over to talk about it tonight. I'd like you to check up on it. Can you do that?"

"So you don't trust him?" Tom squinted at me with a look of suspicion in his eyes.

"It's not that I don't trust him." Then I paused. "Well I guess I don't really trust anybody. I had a problem with trust for most of my life. Being in this job has made me believe everybody has a dark side. Everybody. Axel is probably no different. He had a terrible life growing up in Australia but that doesn't excuse anything. Anyhow, I just want to know for sure that my boyfriend is not involved in anything that's illegal. That's all."

"Okay then. I'll check on it for you. I'll get back with you.

"Thanks, Tom." I took another deep breath. "I love him. I really do. But I have to know the truth."

Tom was quiet for a few minutes.

"What's going on Tom? What are you thinking about?"

"Well, you know how you were saying you never really know people. Right?"

"Right. I mean, it's been my experience that anybody pushed in the wrong direction can be capable of doing anything. Murder in cold blood...whatever..."

Tom didn't say anything. His silence was deafening.

"Tom, are you thinking what I think you're thinking?"

"I don't know, what do you think I'm thinking?"

As I looked at his face, I knew my suspicions were true.

Tom suspected Damien of killing Josh.

CHAPTER 8

"Tom, tell me what's on your mind."

"I just think we have to not shut down any possibilities. If we're looking at Damien's mother for this then we might as well face the possibility that Damien himself might've been involved."

I didn't want to think about that, but I knew he was right. Damien had motive to kill his dad. His fingerprints were on the murder weapon. I couldn't think of any other reason why only his fingerprints were on the murder weapon. It was suspicious that Damien's fingerprints were on the weapon and nobody else's were. The lamp was brand new. Whoever did it had to have known Damien touched the lamp. And then they would had to have bludgeoned Josh with that lamp, using a pair of rubber gloves. Not that any of this was out of the question, because it wasn't. But it was very unusual.

The circumstances were quite unusual.

I wrote it down. "Damien," I said to Tom. "Now I know he was in prison for a number of years and said he was wrongfully convicted. Is there still a possibility that maybe he was involved in the robbery with his buddies?"

"I think he *was* involved in the robbery with his buddies."

"Why do you think that?"

Tom took a sip of his drink and cocked his head. "Why do you suppose Damien's been so anxious to get his buddies out of prison for all these years? He's done so many things to get them out, all of which involved some kind of blackmail. He got Nick, Jack and Tommy out by threatening to expose the system that put him behind bars in the first place. He had very good grounds for a lawsuit, but dropped it in exchange for his buddies having their sentences commuted. That's blackmail. And now look what happened with the dick-pic and Governor Weston. That's also blackmail."

"Okay, so what does that have to do with anything?"

"Are you that naïve?" Tom asked.

"I guess I am. What are you thinking?" I had no idea what was going through Tom's mind, but it wasn't good. He was very good friends with Damien. If anybody could dig up dirt about Damien, it would be him.

Tom shrugged his shoulders. "Now listen, I'm Damien's friend. But I'm a realist too. Aspects of Damien's prison story never rang true with me over the years. Now maybe I'm full of shit, but I've always entertained the possibility that Damien was good for that robbery and got out of prison by some other means."

"What other means?"

"Listen, after Damien told me his story, I went to the newspapers and found the articles about the Innocence Project and how they were involved in Damien's case. The project involved itself in his case and really did free him. I know they did. I understand that. However, I did some digging into his case. I found some pretty interesting things."

"What kinds of things?" I was intrigued by his words yet dreading them all the same.

"Well, the reason why Damien was awarded a new trial was because a witness to the case, the one who fingered him as being part of the robbery, recanted her story."

"Yes, that's true. She was the only one who said he was at the robbery. If she recanted her story, then obviously that was good grounds to have his case reopened."

"Right. But that's not the only thing. They did DNA analysis on the getaway car and the liquor store and found Damien's DNA was nowhere to be found on either of those premises. That's the real reason why he got a new trial. The DNA analysis said he had nothing to do with it, period."

"Yes, that's true," I said.

He took a deep breath. "Listen, I just need for you to talk to Damien about this. See if you get a straight answer from him. He'll tell you because you're his attorney now."

"What kind of story are you looking for?"

"I think Damien was the mastermind behind the entire robbery. He claimed he knew nothing about it. I think he did. He was always the brains behind what the guys did. He was like their leader. I personally don't think something as big as this would've been planned without him being there and giving them the plans to begin with."

"Why are you saying these things to me, Tom? Damien is your friend." Tom was trying to throw Damien under the bus, but why?

Tom just shrugged. "As I said, I'm an investigator. I look at things realistically. I have to look at things with cynical jaded eyes. A cynical jaded eye in this situation would say there's a possibility Damien was not as pristine in the robbery incident as he says. That's all."

"And so you're saying that if he planned the robbery, he could've killed Josh? I still don't understand that connection."

Tom tapped his pen on the table and looked at me thoughtfully. "All I'm saying, Harper, is you should not discount the possibility that maybe Damien did it. It's not just the fact that Josh raped his mother. Personally, I think Damien is upset about that but that's not enough to make him angry enough to do something like this."

"Hold up, hold up, hold up. Are you telling me Damien has a terrible temper? Why do I think you're about to tell me that perhaps Damien did it in the heat of passion? That Josh made him so angry he would do something like that? Is that what you're trying to say?"

"Listen," Tom said. "Damien has a lot of pent-up rage inside of him. You would too if you lived the kind of life he has. He was living on the streets when he was 12 and 13 and so forth. His stepfather was abusive, which is why he left his house. He did things with his friends over the years and it didn't always involve something as simple as stealing. Sometimes it involved getting into some extremely serious fights. I know it's all a matter of his juvenile record, and unfortunately, his juvenile record has been unsealed. I think you take a look at the things he's done. Take a look before you decide it's impossible Damien did this. That's all I'm saying."

I swallowed hard. I didn't want to think Damien would've been behind killing his own father. Or any kind of murder, for that matter.

"Tom, why would you tell me these things? I'm just curious."

"Because Harper, I think you need to face that Damien might've killed his father. If he did it, I think you could get him to tell you. And if you get him to admit it, you could maybe work a good deal for him."

"But what if he did it and I still have to try the case? What about that?"

"It's your job to convince him to take any decent deal that comes his way. If he did it. I'm not saying he did. All I'm saying is you need to look at his juvenile record and see the things he did. Then you can realize what kind of explosive temper he has inside him."

"But what would Josh have done to Damien to make him so angry?"

"Harper, I don't know the answer to that question. I really don't. It's entirely possible that something happened and Josh threatened Damien in some way or worse. Maybe Josh threatened his kids or maybe he threatened the guys." He nodded his head. "After all, the story is that Nick was stealing from Josh and that's why Damien killed him. Damien would kill over something like that. That's all I'm saying."

I sighed. I thought I knew Damien. I thought I knew Axel. But did I really know either man? Was Axel involved with illegal things at his job? Was Damien involved in the murder of his father? Or was his mother involved? I didn't want to think these things were possible even though I'd never met his mother. I didn't want Damien's mother to go to prison after all Damien had gone through in his life. And now, after speaking with Tom, I realized Damien's mother going to prison might be the best-case scenario in this case.

The worst-case scenario was that Damien himself goes to prison for the murder of his father.

And an even worse-case scenario would be that he deserved it.

CHAPTER 9

I left Tom with my thoughts very much out of sorts. All I could think about was Tom urging me to look into Damien's juvenile record, recently unsealed by the governor. What crimes did he commit as a juvenile? I realized I didn't know the answer to that question.

And wasn't there the possibility Damien was the mastermind behind the robbery that sent all his friends to prison? If that was the truth about Damien, that would explain a lot. It would explain why he was so anxious to get his friends out of prison and why he would go through any lengths to do it.

He risked everything for Connor when he blackmailed Governor Weston. Why would he do something like that for Connor? Connor was his friend, I knew that, however I didn't think Connor was his best friend. Nick was probably his best friend. Damien did something that clearly illegal and it might've backfired on him.

I thought about that angle. I thought about how the governor was angry with Damien and how the governor would probably lose his seat because of the Connor commutation. It was entirely possible the governor really had it in for Damien for that reason.

I shook my head as I drove on towards my house. Then I suddenly got the idea to go to the courthouse and look at Damien's juvenile record.

I called the girls. "I'm going by the courthouse and will be home for dinner by six. Axel's coming over tonight. I have to talk to him."

Abby answered the phone. "Okay, Mom. I'll see you when you get home."

I drove to the courthouse intending to look at the records. I was very nervous about it because I didn't really know what I'd find out about Damien. I also wondered how much he admitted to the Missouri Bar when he made his application. The Bar was always looking at the fitness of everybody who would apply to be an attorney in Missouri, and I wondered if he disclosed the information about his juvenile record on the Bar Application.

I didn't think Damien necessarily would be in trouble for not disclosing his juvenile record on the Missouri Bar application. His juvenile record was unsealed at the moment, but at the time when he applied for the Missouri Bar, it was sealed. However, it was clear the character and fitness part of the application asked about juvenile convictions or adjudications. I knew there was a very good chance that, especially since the governor was hot on his ass, Damien could be disbarred for lying about his juvenile record. Ordinarily, it would just be a matter of going before the disciplinary board and probably receiving a light suspension.

In this case, he was in danger of losing his livelihood.

The problem was, I didn't know what I'd find out about him by reviewing his juvenile records. The way Tom talked, it was clear there was at least a possibility his crimes involved some kind of violence. That made me nervous. There was some reason why Tom thought Damien wasn't just *capable* of doing this to his father but he might've actually *done* it.

I went to the courthouse and asked for Damien's records. The lady behind the desk got out the files and gave them to me.

"Here they are. These are Damien Harrington's records."

I took the files to a small desk and perused them. As I looked through the records, I realized many of my initial misgivings were true - Damien seemed to have a very extensive juvenile record. He had one major assault case where he beat up a guy with brass knuckles and sent the guy to the hospital. Apparently, this was some kind of a gang initiation. I didn't even know Damien was in a gang. Then again, I supposed that him being in a gang made sense. After all, when he was very young, he lived on the streets and obviously needed protection.

The next record I reviewed showed Damien also had a juvenile adjudication for arson. I read the Statement of Information to see what the circumstances were around this event. Apparently, when he was a young boy, he set fire to his mother's trailer. I read his interview with the police. He apparently told the authorities he set the fire so his stepfather, Steven Harrington, would leave for good. He told the authorities he figured that if he burned down the trailer, his mother would go to a shelter, he would go with her and Steven couldn't go with them. He said he asked some of his friends on the street and that's what they told him - men weren't allowed into shelters with their wives and sons if the shelter director was told the man was abusive.

That made a perverted kind of sense to me. I imagined Damien, who was apparently only 13 years old at the time of the arson, was desperate and naïve. He wanted to do anything possible to get his stepfather out of the house. I didn't quite know if that was true about the shelter, but I supposed it would be. Steven Harrington wouldn't have been welcome at the shelter if Damien told the director his father was abusive. I supposed that was probably true.

I justified this arson in my mind. I was a criminal defense attorney so I always made excuses for everybody I represented. That made it easier to represent criminals and be more persuasive in front of the jury. That was my strong suit –I always sympathized with my clients. Damien was no different.

I went through the rest of the file. I saw several shoplifting charges and several times when he was convicted for stealing cars. None of this was a surprise. Damien told me he had been in trouble with the law quite often when he was young.

I came across his assault charge. It certainly looked like he had a bad temper. He started a fight with a man by the name of Julian Wise. At first, it seemed like the fight was just a normal fist fight between two guys. Then it escalated into something much worse. Damien put on brass knuckles and sent the kid to the hospital, where he remained for three days. The State of Missouri wanted to try Damien as an adult because the case was serious. However it seemed he had a decent attorney who convinced the prosecutor to try him as a juvenile. Consequently, he didn't serve time in an adult prison for this crime. And, because it was a juvenile case, it had been sealed all these years until just recently.

Well, this isn't looking good. Damien had some demons inside him. Demons that perhaps came out when he found out about his father? That was a possibility. I had to admit it.

And then there was the real kicker.

Damien was charged with murder when he was 15 years old.

CHAPTER 10

MY HEART STARTED to pound as I read the Statement of Information for his murder charge. The victim was Damien's stepfather, Steven Harrington. Apparently, his stepfather had come home drunk one night and beat up Damien's mother. It wouldn't have been a problem if he would've killed his stepfather while his stepfather was beating on his mother - that would've been a clear-cut case of defense of others, which is a justification for murder and would have resulted in a full acquittal. However, that was not the case here. Apparently what happened was that his father had passed out drunk on the couch and Damien shot him in the head while he slept.

I read those words and all I could think about was that Damien was very protective of his mother. Even though he always told me he didn't get along with Olivia because of what she did while he was growing up, it was pretty clear that underneath all the bluster, Damien was very protective of her. That concerned me, to say the least - what if Damien killed Josh because he was protecting his mother?

I carefully read the Statement of Information on the murder case. Once again, it seemed the prosecutor's office wanted to try Damien as an adult. Once again, he had a decent attorney who ensured this didn't happen. He was tried as a juvenile, and, even though he had actually killed his stepfather, in the end he was convicted of assault and given probation.

After I got through reading Damien's juvenile record, I realized one thing. At the very least, Damien would be in serious trouble with the Missouri Bar if he didn't disclose any of these convictions. That's what the governor was probably thinking when he unsealed the records. That was his revenge on Damien for doing what he did with Connor. That was the governor's revenge for putting him in a situation where he had to commute Connor's sentence, which in turn caused the governor's political career to go down the tubes.

But even more than that, it made me question whether or not Damien actually killed Josh Roland. It would make sense to do something like that. He definitely had it in him to kill. He had assaulted Julian Wise when he was 15 and killed his stepfather that same year. Granted, this was all when he was a young boy. I had a hard time judging him about what he had done in his youth. But, then again, if nothing else, these earlier charges and earlier convictions showed me just how much pent-up rage was inside him.

I walked away from the Courthouse that day feeling stunned and out of sorts. I would have contact the attorney he had back in the day, whose name was Marissa Banks. She represented him in his assault charge with the kid and the murder charge with the stepfather. I didn't know how much she could tell me about Damien in those day because of attorney-client privilege, but I could get Damien to waive that and maybe she could fill me in on what I needed to know.

There was also one other person I needed to speak with. It

was the court-appointed psychologist involved in Damien's murder case. I would get Damien's permission to speak with this guy. Hopefully Damien would sign off on waiving the physician's privilege in this case. It was important to me to know just what the psychologist found with regards to Damien and whether or not he was diagnosed with any kind of a mental disorder.

Once I did my background research, I would have to ask him point blank if he killed his father. He would hate me for asking that question, but it was a question I asked all my clients. I needed to know. If I knew he did this, then I'd either plead him out or approach the case in a different way. I'd stop trying to find somebody who might be good for this case.

As I drove, my phone was ringing in the car. I answered it. It was Damien.

"Hello Harper," Damien said. "What are you doing?"

"I was at the courthouse, Damien. I was looking through your juvenile records."

Damien was quiet for a few seconds. "I know what you're thinking. I know you're thinking I might've done this. And I know you know about my history and background."

I wanted to lie to him. I wanted to tell him he was wrong. That I believed in him. But I couldn't bring myself to say these things.

"Damien, I need speak with you in person."

"Come on over. After all, you know where I'll be - I have to either be at this house or at the office. I don't really have a choice. I can't leave the house for anything else. Not even to get groceries. I'm having everything ordered in through a delivery service. It's pretty ridiculous, isn't it?"

"Yes, it's ridiculous." But I was thinking in my head it wasn't ridiculous at all. I was thinking Damien might be dangerous. I never thought that before and hated to think that now.

However, I couldn't help it. It would be one thing if Damien had told me these things before. If he would've just come clean with me before, I would not have been thinking these bad thoughts. But he never told me any of this. I knew why - he was probably very ashamed. Still, the fact that he hid this information made me not trust him.

I drove to his house and knocked on his door. Damien answered it. He looked disheveled, like he didn't comb his hair that day. His hair was dark and curly anyway, so it was kind of wild. He apparently hadn't shaved, either. With his dark complexion and dark hair, his facial hair showed up on his face pretty quickly. He had also lost at least 10 pounds.

He nodded as I walked to the door. "Well, come on in Harper, it's just you and me here. Obviously because the kids are in school right now."

I sat down in one of his leather chairs in his living room. "Damien, I won't lie to you. I'm concerned after reading your juvenile record. Maybe you had it in you to kill your father. I have to treat you like I would treat any other client. That means I have to ask you point blank if you did this."

"Now Harper," Damien said with a smile. "You're better than that. You know that if I told you I killed my father, you couldn't put me on the stand and have me say something different. You know that if I told you I killed him you would have no good options for defending me. You would probably have to plead me out. That's if the prosecutor is willing to give me a plea deal at this point, which is doubtful. So, Harper, even if I killed him, I wouldn't tell you the truth about this."

This was not the reaction I was expecting and was not a reaction I welcomed.

"Damien, don't do this to me."

"Don't do what? You're the one putting me on the spot about this. I'm going to tell you one more time. I did not kill my father. However, I just wanted to make a point that your asking me if I killed my father means you're treating me differently from your other clients. I know you would not demand that information from them. That's all I'm saying."

"You're playing games with me and I don't like it. Just like I want to treat you like you're any other client, treat me like I'm any other attorney. That means you won't run the show. I'm running the show."

Damien hung his head. When he looked at me I could see he was angry. "I guess what really makes me angry is you don't believe me and don't trust me. I told you before I didn't kill him. When I said I didn't kill him it means I didn't kill him. Period."

"I'll just have to take your word for it." I still wasn't comfortable but I had to proceed forward in the belief that he was innocent. "Well, the good news is that, of course, the prosecutor cannot use your prior juvenile record against you in court. Not just because it's a juvenile record but because they can't use prior convictions to impeach you on the stand."

"Well, they might be able to use my convictions in this case. They might get creative and use it to show motive to kill Josh."

"Motive? I don't see how your prior record can be admissible at all."

"What they might say is I killed my stepfather Steven Harrington to protect my mother. And they might establish that was my motive for killing Josh as well. To protect my mother."

"I wasn't aware your mother was in danger from Josh."

Damien was very quiet. Then he quietly shook his head. "No, Harper, I don't think my mother was in danger from Josh. However, there was something else I found out about him that concerns me greatly. I'm going to tell you this even though I don't want to. I don't want you to think this gave me a motive to kill him. It's something I hope the prosecutor doesn't find out about Josh, because if they do, they'll fry me."

I blinked. "Go ahead, Damien, tell me what you have to tell me."

Damien sighed. "Harper, the person who was endangered by Josh was not my mother. It was my daughter."

CHAPTER 11

"Go ahead Damien," I said. "Go ahead and tell me what happened."

"Well, I know I told you I only went to see Josh at his office. However, that was a lie. I don't know why I lied to you about that but I did. I guess because I thought that if I told you this story, you would suspect I killed my father and I don't want you to believe that."

My heart started pounding. "So you lied to me?"

"Yes, I lied to you. I don't know why. I guess I thought maybe you wouldn't find out the truth. I thought maybe you wouldn't find out I was capable of killing somebody to protect someone I love. And I am. You now know I am. So I might as well lay my cards on the table and tell you what happened."

"Okay, go ahead."

Damien took a deep breath. "What you need to know is that my father Josh is a sick fuck. A very sick fuck. But I actually had him over to my house once. I made dinner for him."

"Was your mother there too?"

"No, she wasn't there for that." He paused for a moment

and hung his head. "Oh God, this is very tough to talk about. However, I think you need to know. It's entirely possible the prosecutor already knows about it and they'll give this as motive for killing Josh. If they don't know about it, that's in our favor. Let them present to the jury the theory I killed Josh to protect Nick from prosecution. That will never fly, especially since it seems they're not charging him with anything."

I watched him carefully. He had his head in his hands and looked haunted. He shook his head several times. And then he got up, and started pacing around. "What would you do?" he cried. "He came over here one day, and I didn't even know he was here. Gretchen was watching the kids and I guess she wasn't watching them all that well. My father was here. He went down to the rec room and played video games with my daughter. Or so he told Gretchen. What actually happened was he was downstairs with my daughter and he molested her."

I involuntarily drew a breath. I should've seen this coming, but yet, I didn't. Somehow, this piece of information rocked me to the core, like nothing else I had heard about Josh.

Damien drew a breath. "I didn't know it at the time, Harper. I swear it. All I know is I came home one day and Gretchen told me my father was already there. I asked her what he was doing, and she said he was downstairs playing video games with Amelia. Which struck me as extremely odd, to say the very least. Because trust me on this, my father was not a video game-playing type of guy."

Damien continued, his eyes not meeting mine. "I didn't want to believe anything had happened. So I just went along, and said okay, now he's here, I guess I'll make dinner for him. So that's what I did. Made dinner for him. It wasn't until later that my daughter told me what he did to her."

I suddenly was feeling extremely nervous. "Damien, I understand you were upset with him. That's horrible." I suddenly started to remember how it felt to be violated. How helpless I felt. I couldn't imagine that happening to a young girl. The very thought of that sickened me. "I'm so sorry to hear that."

Damien was still pacing around. "I went to see him that day, I did. I went to see him and was extremely angry." He took a deep breath. His hands flew to his hair and he started to pull on the roots. "I was so angry, Harper. I shouldn't have gone over there to see him when I was that angry. I know I shouldn't have gone to see him." He made a fist and thrust it into the air. "I knew I shouldn't have gone to see him."

"Damien, what happened? What did you do?"

He looked at me and then sat down, his head in his hands. He was quiet for a few minutes. I could hear a pin drop.

Finally, he spoke. "I confronted him. I said I knew what he did. I told him that."

"What did he say to you?"

"What do you think he said? He told me he didn't know what I was talking about. I looked at his smug face and knew he knew exactly what I was talking about. And in that moment, I wanted to kill him. I did, Harper. I wanted to kill him."

I swallowed hard. I didn't want to ask him the next question, but I knew I had to. "You wanted to kill him, Damien? And did you kill him?"

He was quiet for a few minutes. During those minutes, I couldn't breathe. All I could think of was there was a distinct possibility he killed Josh and I couldn't blame him for having done that. If somebody had done that to one of my girls, I probably would've killed that person too. I wouldn't have even thought twice. I would've just done it.

"What happened Damien?"

A huge sigh. "Harper, I didn't kill him. I wanted to. And I will admit that's the real reason why my fingerprints were on that lamp. I saw his smug face and saw red. I was blind with rage. I remember picking up the lamp and I swung it at him. But I checked my swing. I did. I know I did. The lamp never actually hit his head. I just *wanted* to kill him. Honest, Harper. That's what happened. I swear to God that's what happened."

I wanted to believe him but it was just too coincidental. He went in there and swung at Josh with the lamp and then Josh ended up dead because he was bludgeoned by that very same lamp? How could I believe Damien's story? It was just too far-fetched.

"So you swung at him with the lamp but you swear you didn't actually hit him with that lamp. That's what you're telling me Damien?"

"That's exactly what I'm telling you, Harper."

"Is it possible you hit him with that lamp, Damien? After all, you said you were blind with rage. That's what you just told me. You were blind with rage. I've tried enough murder cases in my life to know that sometimes people become temporarily insane. They don't know they've actually killed somebody because they don't remember doing it. And the reason why they don't remember doing it is because they were blind with rage, just like you were that day. Not that I blame you. I'm just saying that it's possible you could've killed him and not even remembered it afterward."

Damien nodded. "I know what you're saying Harper, I do. I, too, have tried enough murder cases to know this happens more than people might want to believe. But it's not that, Harper. What happened in that office was not that. I will admit I was extremely angry with him and I admit I swung the lamp at him, but I will not admit I killed him with that lamp."

My heart was in my shoes. How did Damien know he didn't kill Josh? It was looking worse and worse.

"Well, I will have to say one thing."

"What's that?"

"This case will be a helluva hard one to win."

"I know."

"And Damien, I need to ask you something else."

"What's that?"

I drew a breath. "The robbery the guys were convicted of. Did you have something to do with it?"

He looked surprised I would ask that question. "No, Harper. No, I didn't. I would tell you if I did, especially now that we're covered by attorney-client privilege, but the answer is no. I had no idea they were going to do that. They didn't plan it out, either - it was on a whim. From what I understand, the guys needed money and Tommy just said 'let's hold up a liquor store.' And they did." He paused. "Why do you ask?"

"I just needed to know."

I looked at Damien, who looked so lost, and I knew - no matter how long the odds were, I had to give this case my all.

His life literally depended on it.

CHAPTER 12

I DROVE HOME from Damien's feeling very much out of sorts. I really didn't know what to believe at that point. Damien insisted he didn't kill his father, he only threatened him by brandishing the lamp towards him. Yet Joshua was killed by that same lamp, on the same day Damien was there. It had to be an awful coincidence, unless someone was closely surveilling the office and saw Damien doing that. Then it would be a matter of easily framing him. All they had to do was go in there and use rubber gloves to pick up the lamp and bludgeon Josh with it. That would be a perfect way of framing Damien, because his fingerprints were the only ones on the murder weapon.

But that wasn't my immediate concern. I had to talk to Axel and find out what was going on with him. I was still concerned about what Tasha Bennington told me and had to get to the bottom of it. And I certainly did not like the way he reacted when I asked him about it. I didn't like his evasive answers and how quiet he was when I first brought it up to him. It very much concerned me.

My car drove along the snow-covered streets, and, as I got to my house, I started to feel more and more apprehensive. What would I find out about Axel? He and I had been serious for quite some time. There were even times when I thought I might want to marry him. But if he was keeping a secret like the fact he was corrupt on the police force, I didn't think I could be with him anymore. I couldn't be with somebody who would do something like that. Granted, he didn't seem the type who would do something like that, but as I found out with Damien, you never knew about somebody.

You just never knew.

I got to my house and found Axel was already there. That made me even more nervous. He must've seen me pull up, because he was soon on the porch, his hands dug into the pockets of his jeans. He was as handsome as he had ever been, with his slightly graying temples and beautiful green eyes. I always thought he was the sexiest man I'd ever seen. I wondered if I could look at him the same way after tonight.

"Hello mate," Axel said as I approached the porch. "I thought I'd come here early and wait for you to come home. I've been talking with your kids inside."

I nodded. "Thanks for coming. I really appreciate it." I felt so stiff and weird. Which was something I never felt with him before. I had always felt so relaxed around him - he was my best friend and was somebody with whom I could always just be myself. He had been there for me for through so many different crises.

"Mate," he said. "Before you go inside, I need to speak with you about something. It has nothing to do with what you and I will be talking about later. It has to do with your daughter Abby."

"What about my daughter Abby?"

"I don't know. I just have a feeling there's something going on with her. I have a feeling she might be into something you don't know about. It's just a hunch I have."

"What is that supposed to mean? What do you mean she's into something I don't know about?"

"I just have a feeling she might be experimenting with drugs. It's just a feeling I get by looking at her."

My heart sunk to my shoes. I, too, had a feeling Abby was different, but I just chalked it up to the pain of being an adolescent. "Why do you think that?"

"It's just the way she's acting. Have you noticed she's acting out of character lately? Maybe she's a little short with you and just a little bit temperamental? Are you noticing things like that?"

"Well, actually I have been, but I just figured it was because she's 13 years old and that's what happens when you're 13. You start becoming moody. I mean isn't that the stereotype about kids her age? They're moody? I just think Abby is like that. She's just moody like she's supposed to be at this age."

"I suppose you're right. However, I think there's something else going on with her. You have to understand one thing, Harper - I'm a cop. I've been trained to watch for signs that somebody is into substance abuse, and I just think Abby is. I can see it in her mannerisms and can hear it in her voice. I have a sixth-sense and you need to talk with her about whether or not she's using."

I felt the cold tendril of fear but didn't want Axel to know that. "But I'm her mother. Don't you think I would see the signs she was into drugs?"

"Harper, you're just too close to it. I find that happens a lot. Parents are usually the last to know."

I knew I would have to talk to her about that. And I realized there were now two pressing problems I had, three if you counted the fact that I suspected Damien was good for that murder. "I'll have to worry about this later. For now, you and I have to talk about what I found out from Tasha. She seems to know a lot about you. I think she knew I would be speaking with her, which meant she tried to find out as much dirt about me and the people I loved as possible. She knew she would have to threaten me. Which she did."

Axel hesitated for a long time. His beautiful face turned down and he thrust his hands even further into his pockets. "I know. I know we have to talk about this. And it's something I just did not want to share with you. I'm really sorry about that."

I was suddenly very angry. "Axel, I can't believe you're hiding things from me. I thought we agreed not to hide things from one another."

He sighed. "I know, Harper. I know. Let's go inside. It's pretty cold out here."

We went inside and I saw immediately that Rina and Abby were in the living room playing a video game together. Rina came up to me and gave me a hug but Abby stayed rooted to the floor, playing her game. She didn't even look at me.

I thought about Axel's words. How Axel asked me if she was more moody and irritable than usual. She definitely was. She had been. And Axel, being a cop, certainly was attuned to the signs of drug addiction and abuse. I hoped and prayed that wasn't going on with Abby, but I had to admit she was acting different.

"Hey girls - listen, before dinner, I have to talk to Axel. We're going into the sunroom to talk. I hope you don't mind setting the table and getting things ready for dinner."

"I don't mind," Rina said. "And Abby won't mind either. Right, Abby?"

Abby just shrugged and said nothing. Rina rolled her eyes.

"I'll just speak for her. She won't mind if we have dinner later."

I suddenly knew the person I would have to talk to about Abby was not Abby herself, but Rina. She could give me some hints about what was going on with Abby in school. Rina could also tell me if there was any kind of gossip about Abby - any gossip that suggested the kids were talking about her being on drugs. I knew when I was in school that everybody knew who were the so-called freaks – the kids who would drink and do drugs every day or on the weekends. Rina was always in the know about what was going on in her school.

"Rina, I need to speak with you a little later too."

"What about, Mom?"

"I don't want talk to you about it right now. I want to save it for later. But I need to speak with you."

"Okay, Mom."

Axel and I went into the sunroom and sat down on one of the big easy chairs. It was a chair large enough for the two of us to sit together and cuddle up. It was always one of my favorite chairs – it was soft red leather and reclined. We sat in the chair and I got a blanket from behind us and put it over us.

"Okay, what do you need to talk to me about?" Axel asked me.

"What do you need to tell me? I have to admit I'm afraid of what you're about to say."

Axel sighed, which was the one thing I didn't want to hear from him. I wanted him to give me a full-throated denial that he was at all involved in any kind of corruption on the police force. I needed to hear that from him. But that was not what I was hearing from him at all. I was hearing sighs and silence and all those other little signs my clients always gave me when I knew they were lying to me about something they did.

"Okay Harper," he said. "Here's what I'm hiding from you. I told you before I had a brother named Daniel right? I told you about my mother who was suffering from bi-polar disorder and how she killed herself?"

"Yes, I remember you talking about Daniel. You mentioned you had a brother named Daniel, but I don't think you mentioned where he is or what he does or anything else about him." Come to think of it, I always wondered why Axel never really talked about his brother. I had a feeling maybe the brother suffered from the same kind of problems his mother did. I wondered if that was the case.

"Well, Daniel lives here in America. He lives out in Los Angeles. He's going to be moving to Kansas City soon, though, to be closer to me. And the reason why he wants to move closer to me is because he's suffering from his own problems in Los Angeles. You see, I told you about my mother and her bipolar disorder. I believe Daniel is suffering from the same thing. He doesn't have a diagnosis yet, but has all the hallmarks of it. Just like my mother, he has always tended to go in spurts where he spends a lot of money, gambles and stays up for days on end. During these times he visits a lot of prostitutes. And I recently found out he was into heavy drug dealing out in Los Angeles. I found that out and told him he needed rehab. He not only was dealing drugs but was into drugs. He was doing a lot of them."

"Okay, but what does any of this have to do with what's going on with you on the force?"

Another huge sigh. "Harper, my brother visited about a month ago. I know you don't remember him coming, because I didn't tell you he was here. I'm very sorry Harper, but I just don't want you to meet him just yet."

For some reason that made me very angry. Axel and I were supposed to be in a relationship. Didn't that mean we were supposed to know one another's family and one another's secrets? He knew my family, as crazy as they all were. I didn't feel ashamed about him meeting them. Yet he apparently felt ashamed about his brother and did not want me to meet him. That hurt.

"Okay, Axel. So he was here and you didn't even tell me he was here. That's great, just great."

"Harper, I was concerned for you. You were having a hard time with your own sobriety. I didn't want you around a fellow addict at the time. I was afraid he would influence you and not in a good way."

I didn't know if Axel told the truth, but it made perfect sense to me after he said that. It made perfect sense because he was right about one thing – addicts tend to feed off one another. That was why whenever an addict is trying to become clean, they always say "change your playground and your playmates." It was obvious why that was always the biggest piece of advice for drug addicts trying to get clean. If you don't change your playmates, you'll get right back into it because they're all still doing it and you'll want to do it too. It was human nature to want to blend in with your environment. If you're around other addicts you'll inevitably go back to your bad habits.

"But you said he was into drugs and I've never been into drugs." That was all I could think to say. That was a dumb argument and I knew it. I just didn't want to admit Axel was right and I was wrong.

"Yes, he is into drugs. He also is a severe alcoholic. I'm sorry, Harper, I was only looking out for you."

I wanted to believe him. "Okay, Axel, I believe you. Now tell me what his visit has to do with what's happened to you on the force?"

He got very quiet. "When he was here, he was dealing drugs and was arrested. He was arrested by a mate of mine on the force, whose name is Officer Tindell.

"Okay, go ahead. He was arrested here in Kansas City. So what does that have to do with anything?"

"Well, here's what happened. After he was arrested, I realized he was in a lot of trouble. He was arrested for dealing. When the police raided his place at the seedy east-side motel where he was staying, they found he had pounds of cocaine, heroin and meth in that hotel room. They were going to upgrade the charges to federal charges. I knew if that happened, he would be going to prison for a long time."

"And yet he's in Los Angeles now. Why? Why is he in Los Angeles? He had all those drugs on him which would mean, at the very least, he'd be going to trial. Probably he would already be in prison."

Axel took a deep breath and hung his head. "I did something really bad. I shouldn't have done it. I know I shouldn't have. And I just can't believe Tasha Bennington found out about this because I didn't think anybody knew about it. But what happened was I went into the evidence room and stole all the drugs we confiscated from him."

My heart stopped when he said that. "And what did you do with them?"

"I didn't do a thing with them, I promise. Well, actually, that's a lie. I did something with them. I flushed them down the toilet. All of it. So, the upshot was, we no longer had any evidence my brother was dealing drugs. All the evidence was literally flushed down the toilet. Once the evidence went missing, our office had no choice but to drop the charges against him. And that's what happened."

"And nobody knows about this?" I was incredulous.

"No, I didn't think anybody knew. I was on the surveillance tape, but I destroyed that part of the surveillance tape. I got a hacker to do that for me." He hung his head. "I thought I was in the clear, but apparently I'm not. Tasha knows about it. I wonder who else does?"

"I wonder how Tasha knows about it if nobody else does.

But yes, she seems to know about what happened." Then again, maybe she didn't know anything. Maybe she was bluffing. That was a possibility, I had to admit.

"The only thing I can think of is the hackers I hired to destroy that part of the surveillance tape work for her as well. Or there is some other way Tasha found out about it? Do you think she's the only person who knows about it?"

It made sense the hackers might be in Tasha's pocket. If that was the case, Axel could be safe. Those hackers wouldn't turn Axel in after he hired them. Turning on people who hired them would be an excellent way for them not to be hired in the future by anybody. If there was one thing I knew about mercenary hackers – they were tight-lipped about their clients.

"I suppose so, because if somebody else knew about it, you would've already been arrested." I shook my head. "Why would you do something like that? Seriously, Axel, why would you do something like that? I don't understand." I suddenly realized it was true - I didn't really know Axel after all. I had always known him to be an upstanding decent ethical guy, and now, suddenly, he was showing his true colors.

"I don't know," Axel said. "All I know is I panicked. I knew my brother would face serious charges, and knew it was just a matter of time before the Feds got involved and my brother would be spending the rest of his life in prison. I panicked. You have to understand, Harper, it's just Daniel and me. We're the last of the Springers. I always promised my mum I would take care of him. I promised her that. She was always so concerned about him because she knew the signs. She knew he was suffering from the same disorder she was suffering from. And she was always scared for him. I felt I failed him."

"How did you fail him?"

"I failed him because I abandoned him."

That made little sense to me. "How did you abandon him?"

"Well, when Daniel and I came to America, I knew he was having problems. I knew he was having the same kind of problems my mum had and I didn't do anything for him. I tried. I did. However, he chose to move out to Los Angeles and I had to live here. I would university here and met my ex-wife here. Daniel lived with me for a while, here in Kansas City, and I tried very hard to make sure he stayed clean and sober. It was a full-time job for me. But I lost track of him when he went to Los Angeles."

"Why did he go to Los Angeles in the first place?" I was softening towards Axel. I saw his pain and saw he felt he had no choice. He was the same as anybody else, really – he went above and beyond to protect the person he loved. That fact didn't make what he did okay but it was a little understandable.

"He went to LA because he felt stifled here," Axel said. "Bored. He wanted to live on the West Coast because he loves the ocean. The beach. When we lived in Australia, we lived by the beach. And Daniel was always surfing. He wanted to become a professional surfer when he was younger. So he decided to live in Los Angeles to surf and be part of the beach scene. When he went out to Los Angeles, I lost track of him. I didn't visit him and didn't call him anymore. I became so involved with my life, that, I hate to say it, but for a while there, I tried to pretend I didn't have a brother. He was a source of stress for me and I didn't want to think about him."

"And so you felt responsible for his drug problems?"

"Yes, in a way I felt that way. I should've known he had problems just like my mum and should've been more diligent about making sure he got the help he needed. So what happened when I destroyed the evidence, and the charges were dropped against him, is I told him what I did. And threatened him. I said that if he didn't come out here and live in Kansas City so I could be close to him, I would make sure I got the evidence back to the cops and he would be arrested again. Of course, that was an empty threat, because I got rid of that evidence as soon as I could. But it worked and he's going to be living out here soon."

"But Axel, even if he lives out here, there's no way you can just babysit him. Right?"

"Yes, that's true. I found a house close to mine so I can check on him a lot more often. I feel we have a second chance. I don't want to blow it this time. I want to make sure he's clean and sober. I also want to make sure he doesn't go back into drug dealing. And there's no way I can monitor that if he lives in Los Angeles and I'm living here."

"Well, it's safe to say that if anybody ever found out what you did with those drugs, you would be arrested. To say the very least."

"I know that. I just can't believe somebody knows about it. I'm freaked out by that. I don't know what evidence Tasha has, but she could sink me."

"Well, I guess it goes without saying I won't call her to the stand because if I did, she would go to the cops about what she knows about you." I shook my head. "I just can't believe you did something like this. Not that I don't understand it. I do understand it. But it was a crazy thing for you to do. And you could be in a lot of trouble." I paused. "And because you did something like that, it has tied my hands with Tasha. Granted, she threatened to plant evidence on me and make sure I also got arrested. However, I think if it weren't for what you did, I probably would've rolled the dice and subpoenaed her to trial. She knows things about Josh that will be extremely illuminating, things that could get my client off for murder."

"I'm so sorry, Harper." Axel looked devastated and my heart went out to him. He knew what he did was wrong. He probably didn't ever imagine his actions would have ramifications for my client and me. His actions did have these ramifications and that affected him greatly.

I drew a breath. "Axel, I just need some time to process all this. I'm having trouble with it."

"I knew you would if you found out what I did. I understand you'll need some time with this. So I guess I'll be leaving." He looked at me with his green eyes looking very hopeful and I felt terrible. He was clearly waiting for me to ask him to stay but I was at war with myself. I loved this man so much, but I would have to figure out if he was the type of guy I wanted to be with. He did something terrible and I knew he had his reasons for it, but I didn't know if those reasons were good enough.

I could tell he was wanting me to beg him to stay or at least ask him. But I didn't want to do that. I not only didn't want to necessarily be around him, but I also knew I would have to talk with Abby. That was one conversation I didn't want to have.

After a few minutes of silence between us, which no doubt led Axel to believe I wouldn't try to keep him there with me, he finally just shook his head, stood up, and headed towards the French doors of the sunroom. "Harper, I'll be in touch with you soon."

I nodded and said nothing.

At that, he left.

I didn't talk to Abby that night. I was too in my head about what Axel had just told me and was feeling very emotional about it. I didn't want to add even more misery onto my evening so I decided not to speak with her.

I put off speaking with her that night, but it was something I would have to tackle.

Sooner rather than later.

CHAPTER 13

THE NEXT DAY I knew I had to get back on Damien's case. So I decided to make an appointment with Tom to see if he'd found out anything pertinent about the investigation he could let me in on.

We met at the same bar we met at before. He was already there, drinking a beer. As usual, I felt the twinge of wanting to share a beer with him. It was always my thing. I always felt like being social with somebody and that meant having a drink with them. But I was still on the wagon, and there was no way I would get off it again. My sobriety was too hard-fought.

"So what you got for me?" I asked Tom.

"Well, I found out something extremely interesting to me. Extremely interesting to me."

"What? What did you find out?"

"I found out Damien's ex-wife Sarah was connected to Josh Roland."

"What do you mean? How was she connected to him?"

"Here's what I found out. She's known for years that Josh Roland was Damien's father. Apparently Damien's mother,

Olivia, told her many years ago about his father. And Olivia swore her to secrecy."

"Okay, and? What am I missing here?"

"Here's what you're missing. Sarah got to know Josh. I guess she was curious and wanted to find out more about him. She wanted to tell Damien about Josh being his father but wanted to see what kind of person Josh was. At least, that's what I gather from speaking with Olivia. That's what she told me."

"Okay, what you're saying, basically, is that Sarah was like a scout trying to determine if Damien should get to know his father. Is that what you're telling me?"

"Yes, that's what I'm telling you."

This was getting interesting. Very interesting. "What happened?"

"Well, as you probably know, Sarah is a very attractive woman. Extremely attractive. And she's just Josh's type. Blonde hair, tall, thin, gorgeous rack. And, you might imagine what happened next."

"I don't think I have to imagine what happened next, but go ahead."

"Well, here's what happened. He hit on her. Apparently she said no, and when she did, he hit her."

"This is what Olivia told you? He hit Sarah?"

"Yes, that's what happened. He got extremely angry when she turned him down."

"What was the ruse she had to meet him? She didn't tell him she was trying to get to know him because he was Damien's father did she?" I asked.

"No. Apparently she went to work for him. He hired her as an assistant and she worked for him for several months. Damien knew she was working but never knew where. You have to remember, she's a schoolteacher and would get jobs during the summer time. She worked for him one summer.

Olivia said that was Sarah's way of doing a deep dive into who Josh was. And it worked. He took her out to dinner one night. He apparently had too much to drink and told her how beautiful she was. And then he invited her to his hotel room. She refused to go but that didn't deter him. He gave her a ride home in his limo and tried to take off her clothes. She fought him and he hit her. And he also fondled her by putting his fingers where they're not supposed to be. When he did that, she kicked him with her high heels. And that caused him to hit her again."

As he was speaking, I felt cold tendrils go up and down my spine. I thought about Michael and how he made me helpless. Sarah apparently was in the same position. She, too, was helpless. She was in the limo with this creep and he sexually assaulted her. This was the same sick guy molesting Damien's six-year-old daughter. He was very much a sick man.

"Okay, so I'd imagine after that, Sarah told him she would no longer work for him. That goes without saying, doesn't it?"

"Hell yes that goes without saying. And Sarah also told Olivia she would never tell Damien who his father was. He was the same sick person Olivia knew all those years ago."

I nodded, thinking this was definitely a good lead. "I need to talk to her. I need to find out what she knows. There's a good chance maybe she did this. After all, she has it in for Josh and also has it in for her ex-husband right? So she was not only angry enough to kill Josh but also angry enough with Damien to ensure he went down for this."

There was only one snag. I still had to figure out how the person, whoever it was, knew Damien was in there earlier, brandishing that lamp like a weapon. The real killer had to have known that. I would have to get a court order to have the place swept for some kind of surveillance equipment. That was the only thing I could think of- somebody had some kind of surveillance equipment in the office and could monitor the situation. And then, when they saw Damien had swung the lamp, knew it was their chance to finish Josh off with that same lamp. That way they knew Damien would be arrested for it.

"Okay, thank you very much for this. Is there anything else you found out during your investigation?"

"Well, I found out what Josh was doing. He was habitually a sexual harasser of his female employees. Josh hired only the most attractive women. He would always call them to his office and do things while they were there. He would masturbate in front of them and would chase them around and try to get their clothes off. He would send his female employees sexually suggestive texts and naked pictures. He would have his female employees in his office and would lock the doors. Then he would try to kiss them and would attack them. And, every once in a while, he would actually get an employee who would actually go to hotel rooms with him and they'd have sex."

"And what did you find out about how he got away with this behavior?"

"It's pretty simple. There were always lawsuits against him but he settled immediately. And the media never found out about it because of Tasha's intervention. She did her job very well in covering up what he did. Nobody ever knew about it except the women themselves. And, of course, human resources knew about the incidents, because they, too, were involved in covering it up."

"I need to figure out if maybe one of those women were involved with this," I said. "Here's what I'm thinking. Somebody put a bug in his office and has been surveilling him ever since. Maybe they did that because they were trying to catch him and have evidence against him. And then when Damien did that with the lamp, they saw an opportunity to kill Josh and frame Damien."

"That sounds like a good theory. If you can figure out who had cause to surveil Josh, you might have your killer."

"Ah, there's the rub. That'll be the hard part, won't it?"

Tom smiled. "That's why you get paid the big bucks – to solve these hard parts. I have faith in you. You'll find out who did it."

I was quiet for a few minutes as I sipped my soda water. "But, Tom, you told me the other day you thought Damien did it. Right?"

He shrugged. "I guess so. I still think it's a possibility. But I'm starting to think other people are better possibilities. It's your job to figure out the best candidate."

I smiled. "That's why I get paid the big bucks."

CHAPTER 14

Before I decided to dig into the case, I saw Damien's therapist from when he was 15 years old. Damien signed a release of medical records and a release that let me speak with Dr. Spacey. He told me he had nothing to hide and wanted me to speak with his shrink. I understood the therapist was ordered by the court after Damien was convicted both for the arson and his stepfather's murder.

I went to his office which was by my office on The Plaza. It was on the third floor of a Spanish-style building right by The Plaza movie theaters. He was expecting me so I didn't have to wait long to see him.

Dr. Spacey was a slight man, only about five foot seven and a hundred and thirty pounds. He was blonde and bespectacled and walked with a slight stoop of his shoulders. He nodded his head when his assistant led me back to his office.

"Come in, come in," he said. "You are Ms. Ross I presume?"

"Yes I am."

"And you wanted to speak with me about Damien Harrington?"

"Yes. I am representing Mr. Harrington on a current murder case."

He motioned to the couch. "Have a seat."

I sat down.

"Help yourself to some water."

There was a pitcher on a stand with cucumber water and I fixed myself a glass and sipped. It was tart and refreshing.

He nodded again. "I've been reviewing his file, because you called me earlier today and my secretary told me you would be coming in. What would you like to know?"

I took out my yellow pad and started writing. "I understand you evaluated Mr. Harrington when he was 15 years old. Is that correct?"

"Yes, that's correct." He nodded again. "He was brought to me by the court. I was appointed to be his therapist. It seemed the prosecutors in this case were looking for a reason not to charge him with murder. I think they felt sorry for him."

"They felt sorry for him? Why would they feel sorry for him?"

"They knew Steven Harrington. They knew what kind of person he was. From what I understand, Mr. Harrington was well known by the prosecutors. Over the years, he was arrested many times for assault on his various girlfriends and their children. He was in and out of jail for these assaults and even served a couple of prison sentences for these incidents. For instance, he served five years in prison for first degree assault of a woman whom he was dating. What happened in that case was they were driving in a car, they got into a fight and he pushed her out of the speeding car. She almost died. That's the kind of thing he was constantly in trouble for. The prosecutors knew his number, so to speak."

As he was speaking, I started to feel better about Damien. "Okay, so the prosecutors felt sorry for him. And you think the reason why you were brought into the case was because they were looking for a reason not to charge him with killing his stepfather?"

"Yes, that's what I believe. If I were to guess, I would think the prosecutors in that case were just relieved somebody took care of the guy. Yet they couldn't just not charge Damien with killing his stepfather. After all, Steven Harrington had living parents. Granted, his father was also serving time in prison for assault. And his mother was a drug addict. Regardless, as long as the victim had living family members, it's the unspoken rule in the prosecutor's office to charge all criminal perpetrators."

"So, it's your opinion that if he didn't have a living mother and a father, they might not have even charged Damien with assault?"

"No, I think they would have charged him with assault but not murder. You see, the original charges against Damien was murder in the second degree. What I believe is the prosecutors were looking for reasons to downgrade the charges to assault. And that's where I came in."

"I understand he had an attorney by the name of Marissa Banks. What do you know about her?"

"She's an attorney in the juvenile office and I think she's very good. She's very passionate about what she does. So her being on the case certainly helped Damien as well."

"How many times did you meet with Damien?"

"According to my notes, I met with him five times over the course of three months."

"And do you understand why you were supposed to be evaluating him?"

"Well, it was all part of the prosecutor's office downgrading the charges against Damien. I was to evaluate his frame of mind when he killed his father. As you know, *mens rea* is very important in these cases. I needed to find out if he formed the requisite intent to kill his father and if he did it in cold blood."

I made notes while he spoke. "And what did you determine?"

"I determined Damien at that time was suffering from a version of what is known in the law as battered spouse syndrome. Of course he wasn't the spouse of Steven Harrington, but the child. However, Missouri law does not allow for battered child syndrome. I don't know why that is, it's something I've advocated for years. If there is a defense a battered spouse can bring, there should also be one for the child." He shrugged. "But I don't make laws."

I knew something about battered spouse syndrome. I had represented women before and used that defense in their cases. Missouri recognized the defense. It was a way of getting women acquitted if their spouse had been habitually beating on them for a period of time. In the State of Missouri, you can use evidence the person was suffering from battered spouse syndrome when deciding if the person acted lawfully in self-defense or defense of another.

"So," I said. "You came to the conclusion that Damien was suffering from battered spouse syndrome, applied to him as a child?"

"Yes I did. He explained to me that his stepfather had beaten him so badly he had gone to the hospital several times and the stepfather did not beat on his mother as much. He told me he knew what his stepfather was capable of and was afraid his stepfather would kill his mother. He also said he was terrified of him, which was why he shot him in the head while he was sleeping on the sofa. He didn't feel he could have defeated him if the guy was not asleep."

"Okay, so you found Damien acted reasonably in killing his

stepfather? And by that, I mean he acted as a reasonable person would in his situation."

"In a sense, yes, he acted reasonably. He saw his mother wouldn't get rid of the guy and didn't kick him out, even though he was continually beating on him and seriously injuring him. Damien had left the house several times, but was always picked up and brought back. I don't know why social services didn't get involved in the situation, especially because Damien was continually being brought into the hospital with serious injuries. I know hospital personnel and doctors are required to report when they suspect abuse, and I just don't know why Damien's case slipped through the cracks as much as it did. That's a mystery to me. What I know is that Damien was terrified of his stepfather, and really thought his stepfather would kill his mother."

"Now, I need to ask another question. As you know, Damien is currently on trial for killing his birth father, Josh Roland."

"Yes, I understand that."

"Is it your professional opinion that Damien killed his stepfather to protect his mother?"

"Yes, I believe that was why he killed Mr. Harrington."

I didn't want to ask him if he thought Damien would kill his father for much the same reason he killed his stepfather – because he wanted to defend his mother.

But I want to find out if the therapist thought Damien was suffering from some kind of mental issue back then. It would be relevant to me because it was entirely possible that maybe Damien was suffering a form of PTSD. If he thought Josh Roland would harm his mother, that might've brought him back to what happened with his stepfather all those years ago, and that would cause him to want to kill Josh.

"Did you diagnose him with any kind of mental disorder?"

"No, I did not. I simply thought he was a young boy afraid for his mother who felt helpless in the situation. He felt like the only thing that could be done, to make sure Steven Harrington did not harm his mother or him anymore, was to kill him. That was my conclusion. And that was why the prosecutors decided not to try him as an adult, and why they decided to not try him for the murder. They simply offered assault to his lawyer Marissa and she thought that was a pretty good deal."

I nodded. This was good news. "It would concern me if you thought Damien had some kind of lasting mental damage from what happened with his mother and Steven. If that were the case, then it would be much more likely, in my opinion, that Damien would be prone to want to kill his father Josh. Thank you very much. I do appreciate your taking time out to speak with me."

"Well, I hope I helped you."

"You did. More than you know."

And as I got into the car, I knew that was correct.

He did help me more than he could possibly know.

CHAPTER 15

When I got home, I knew I would have to talk to Abby. The things that Axel said were burned in my brain and I was obsessing about them just a little.

Abby was not in the living room when I got home, but Rina was. Rina gave me a look and I knew something was wrong. Axel's intuition was probably spot on, and I didn't quite know what to do about it.

"Rina, why are you are you looking like that?"

"Like what, Mom?"

"Like you've seen a ghost." That was the only way I could possibly describe the way she was looking at me – like she had seen a ghost. Her eyes were wide and her face was pale. I looked at her hands and they were shaking.

"Why are you looking like this?" I asked again.

She shrugged. "I don't know what you're talking about."

"I think you know exactly what I'm talking about. Out with it."

She took a deep breath. "Something's wrong with Abby. I don't know what. She won't talk to me."

It was then I heard the screaming upstairs. It was a howl, almost - that was the best way to describe what I heard coming from her room. Howling. It was almost inhuman.

It certainly did not sound like Abby.

I ran up the stairs, almost tripping on the top stair.

"Abby! Abby!" I tried her doorknob, but she had locked the door. "Abby, what's going on in there?"

I heard nothing but more howling and then loud music coming from the computer. She turned it up so loud I couldn't hear her howling anymore. I put my ear to the door and heard her faintly. It was almost drowned out by the music, however. It was some kind of death metal music, not at all like the music she usually listened to. For as long as I'd known her, she was a girl who got into the latest pop groups. Your Taylor Swifts, your Britney Spears, your Harry Styles, your Ed Sheerans, your Beyoncés. Acts like that. I had never heard her play death metal until that moment in time.

"Abby!" I shouted, "you have to let me in."

I heard nothing except her music turned up even louder.

I finally got a crowbar I had kept in the shed out back. I went back up to her room and pried the door open.

When I got in there, I could see she was looking really sick. That was the best word to describe it. Sick. Her dark hair was drenched with sweat. Her brown eyes were as wide as saucers. Her pupils were extremely dilated. She had a glassy stare. It was almost as if she had not seen me. And then she started to howl again. She started scratching her arms and then started screaming about bugs underneath her skin.

I swallowed hard. I knew what all this meant. It meant Axel was actually spot-on. He knew Abby was taking drugs. I didn't know how he knew, but he knew.

"Abby," I said. "You need to talk to me."

She still looked as if she didn't even know who I was. She

had the glassy stare of somebody in their own world. I looked over at Rina who was shaking her head.

"What's wrong with her?" Rina asked.

"I think we need to get her to the hospital. In fact, I know we do."

I didn't quite know how to get Abby into the car to take her to the hospital. By this time, she'd gotten wild. She got on top of her bed and started dancing wildly and shaking her head to the music. I turned the music down. When I did that, she started to scream again.

I decided the only way to get her into the hospital was to call 911. So I did.

I tried to talk to her, but there was no use doing that. I didn't know what she was taking, but it was obviously something.

In a matter of minutes, the ambulance was at our front door. They rushed into her room, and, over her protests, gave her a sedative and strapped her to a gurney. My 13-year-old daughter was being wheeled out on a gurney and put in the back of an ambulance.

Rina and I followed along behind the ambulance in my car.

I called Axel while I drove. "Axel, you were right."

"What was I right about?"

"You're right about Abby. She's definitely on drugs. I'm going to the hospital now because she's out of control. She was screaming, her eyes are wild, her pupils are dilated. And she's high as a kite."

"I'm on my way, mate. Which hospital are you going to?"

"Menorah. I'll be in the emergency room."

As I hung up the phone with Axel I had mixed emotions about him coming to the hospital to see Abby. On the one hand, I knew he could be a great source of comfort and support for me. Not to mention Rina. On the other hand, however, I didn't quite know how I felt about his confession about what he did at the police station. It didn't really concern me, but it scared me that he was capable of doing something like that. Even to save his brother.

I got to the hospital and went into the ER waiting room. Soon after we got there, Abby's treating doctor came out to tell me what they were about to do.

Thirty minutes later, Axel came through the door and I immediately felt comforted. Axel did something very bad, there was no getting around that. But there was also no getting around that I loved the man, warts and all. If push came to shove and he got caught for what he did, I would be behind him 100%. I would even be his lawyer if he asked me to. He was always there for me and I would be there for him. I just hoped it didn't come to that.

"So what's going on with Abby?" he gently asked.

"She's out of control. I'm going to talk with her when she comes to. They've given her a sedative and taking her vital signs. The doctor just spoke with me and said they're probably going to induce vomiting and give her charcoal to absorb the drugs. Then they're going to give her an IV and just wait for her to come down. After that, I'm going to do the hard work. I'm going to..."

All at once, I was crying. I didn't even know exactly where the tears were coming from. Before Axel got there, I was sitting calmly in the waiting room with Rina by my side. I was holding Rina's hand and she was looking really stressed out. She was holding my hand tightly and was putting her head on my shoulder. She was moaning softly. She kept saying she felt bad about what happened, she knew Abby was experimenting with drugs, and kept saying she was sorry for not saying anything about it. I kept telling her it was okay and I needed her to always confide in me. She said she didn't want to confide in me because she felt like she was tattling on Abby, and of course I had to tell her not to ever think that. She must never think she was tattling on Abby, especially on something like this. I know she wanted to protect Abby and I understood that more than anything. I did the same thing for my siblings growing up. But this was too important, I told her. This is too important to keep from me.

But my tears were not only for Abby - they are also tears of guilt. I had to admit that. I'd let Abby down. Axel could see what was going on. Why couldn't I? Was I too close to it? Or was I just too busy? That's what I had to come to terms with. Really. The fact I had let my daughter get this far, without even noticing, because I was too wrapped up in my own life. Too wrapped up with my work and everything else going on around me.

I had to admit my failure.

Axel put his arm around me as I cried. "Mate," he said. "Don't blame yourself. Trust me when I tell you the signs of drug abuse are subtle and you can't always put a finger on it."

"But I should've seen it. I should've seen what was going on. I just saw she was having problems and just figured it was problems that come with being 13 years old. When you're that age, you have issues. I know I did when I was her age. And I just hoped it was something she would grow out of. But apparently it wasn't."

"It's okay. You caught it in time. Hopefully."

"Maybe. I don't know if I caught it in time or not. It might've already gone too far. I might have to send her to rehab." I shook my head. "Oh Axel, I just don't know what to do."

"The only thing you can do is to be there for her. Make sure she gets the help she needs and stay on her."

Axel and I sat in the waiting room for several hours before the doctor came out and spoke with us. "As you know," he said, "your daughter is suffering from a drug overdose. From what we can see in her blood test, it seems she is suffering from an acute heroin overdose."

My heart stopped. Not my daughter. Not my little Abby. Not my sweet Buttercup. I couldn't imagine she would ever do something like that.

I didn't know what to say. I opened my mouth but no words would come out. So Axel did the talking.

"So, when will she be out of the woods?" he asked.

"Well, at the moment she's resting comfortably. We induced vomiting, gave her a saline solution to rehydrate her, and charcoal to absorb the drugs. This is the most we can do for her right now, other than just let her rest comfortably. We will be admitting her into the hospital overnight for observation."

"Can I stay with her?" I asked.

"Yes, you can."

"Axel, can you take Rina home?"

"No!" Rina protested. "I want to stay with her too."

"But Rina, I don't think you can stay with her."

"Why not? You're staying with her. Why can't I stay with her too?"

I looked at the doctor and the doctor nodded. "You may both stay with her tonight. I understand you want her to have a private room."

"Yes, I want her to have a private room. I'd like a room where preferably there's a couch."

"We do have one such room available on the fifth floor. We'll be transferring her to that room overnight."

"Thank you."

As the doctor, whose name was Dr. Green, left, I looked at Axel. "Thank you for coming. I'm going to stay with Abby tonight. I guess Rina will be too. I'll be in touch."

Axel nodded. I knew he had work to do, otherwise he probably would have insisted on staying as well.

"Mate," he said. "She'll be okay."

As I thought about my own addictions, I shook my head. I was addicted to alcohol for years and it was the hardest thing in the world to kick. And now Abby was apparently on heroin. I knew she was addicted and I knew something about that drug. I knew it was one of the most, if not the most, addictive drug on the planet.

Whatever was happening, I knew I'd have a long road ahead.

CHAPTER 16

The next day, I had to leave Abby at the hospital. I needed to work on Damien's case, while, somehow, making sure I was also there for Abby. When I left, she was resting comfortably.

"I'll be back later, Buttercup," I said softly. "I love you."

I took Rina home and made sure she changed her clothes and got something to eat. Then I dropped her off at school and made my next appointment, which was with Marissa Banks, Damien's attorney back in the day. I wanted to see her for the same reason I went to see Dr. Spacey. I basically wanted to get a handle on what was going on with Damien when he killed his stepfather at the age of 15. The doctor seemed to believe that it was something situational. And I took comfort in that. However, I wanted to get another perspective on what was going on with him.

At the moment, Marissa was working in private practice. She had a Midtown office in her residence. It was an attractive home, made of brick with pillars out front. On her lawn was a sign that said *Marissa Banks Attorney at Law*.

I walked onto her porch and knocked on her door.

She answered the door and invited me in. "You must be Harper Ross," she said as she shook my hand. "And you're here to speak to me about Damien Harrington, right?"

"Yes, that's correct." I stepped into her home which was very cute. She had hardwood floors in her living room, and to the right was a small office. She had files everywhere in that room – piled on her desk and on the floor next to her desk. There were also boxes and boxes of files. She evidently did not have an assistant like I did. Pearl was worth her weight in gold, really. If it weren't for Pearl, my office would look very similar to Marissa Banks's office. I was not a natural record-keeper and was not very organized either.

"Excuse the mess," she said. "I have so many cases coming down the pike, I feel like I don't know if I'm coming or going."

"Oh, I know the feeling. I know the feeling very well." I was thinking to myself I not only knew the feeling of having a lot of cases on my plate, but also having a lot of cases on my plate while I had a daughter addicted to drugs.

She hastily took some of her files off her desk, threw them on the floor and then clasped her hands in front of her and looked me in the eye. She was an attractive woman with frizzy blonde hair and big brown eyes. She was probably around 50 years old, which meant she was in her early 30s when she took Damien's case.

"So, what can I do for you?"

"I wanted to ask you some questions. You were Damien's attorney back when he was 15, right? As I understand it, you were on the case when he was accused of arson, right? And again when he murdered his stepfather?"

"Yes, that's right. Apparently, he had set fire to their trailer home while his stepfather was inside. That was the first time he got arrested."

"And he was convicted of that, correct?"

"Yes, he was adjudicated for that."

"And from what I understand, he was placed on probation? It seemed like a pretty serious crime. Do you know why he was given probation?"

"Yes, I do know why."

"And why was that?"

She sighed. "Listen, Harper, there's one thing you have to understand. Steven Harrington was not a nice man. Even so, it was a very serious thing that Damien did. He didn't have a record at the time, aside from some minor things such as shoplifting. I understand that a little bit later on in his life he stole some cars. And was involved with an assault. But this crime was his first felony. So the prosecutors went easy on him."

"And what did you think about Damien at the time?"

"Could you be more specific?"

"Did anything strike you about him emotionally?"

She looked like she was thinking. She put her hand on her chin and tapped her pencil on the desk. "Well, I think he was a very frustrated and angry young person. That's what I got from him."

"What made you believe he was frustrated and angry?"

"You're a lawyer. You know what I'm talking about. He would come into my office and start yelling at the top of his lungs about what was going on. His body language was that of a caged jungle cat. Yes, that's the best way to describe it. A caged jungle cat. Frustrated. Coiled. Ready to strike."

"Did he make you nervous?"

"No, not any more than any of my other clients."

I knew what she was talking about. I had clients accused of everything under the sun. I represented plenty of people who had been arrested for first degree murder. Others who had been accused of robbery and arson. I did not take any sex crime cases, but when I was working for the public defender's office, I did. I had to. There was no way I would ever voluntarily defend somebody accused of rape. Not after what had happened to me.

If you did this job for long enough, you could always tell when somebody was a very angry person.

"Why do you ask these questions?" she asked.

"Well, I'm just trying to know who he is. I mean, I work with him. He's my associate. I would like to offer him a partnership in the event he beats this case. However, I need to know what kind of person he is. I mean, I know him, but only superficially. I see him coming to work and he seems to be in good spirits every single day. I know he's had a lot going on in his life, between getting a divorce, his daughter being sick and being wrongfully imprisoned for five years. So, I just wanted to see what you thought about him when you represented him."

She shook her head. "I didn't think he was out of the ordinary as far as anger management goes. You have to understand - I was working the worst cases in the juvenile division. I was working cases like Damien's – the assaults, the robberies, the arsons, the murders. I wasn't working the theft cases and the drug cases and things like that. Because I was representing the most serious crimes, I was meeting individuals like Damien. He didn't seem to stand out to me, to be honest with you."

I felt cheered after speaking with her. I thought that while Damien had some problems when he was young, it didn't seem as if he had anything deep-seated emotionally and mentally.

"Thank you for seeing me."

"No problem," she said.

I didn't really know what to think after talking to Marissa and talking to Dr. Spacey. What I didn't know was if Damien's issues were such that they would have carried over into his adult life. Damien had always seemed to me to be very level-headed and somebody who could handle life as it threw curve balls at him. And, after speaking with his doctor and his attorney from back when he was 15 years old, I knew my hunch was probably correct. That meant that hopefully I could trust him when he said he did not kill his father.

Now, of course the problem was trying to find out who actually did kill his father.

CHAPTER 17

That same day, I went to Olivia's trailer to speak with her. Somehow, I knew talking with her would be important. If anybody would have the answers I was looking for, it would be her.

Her trailer was in a trailer park in Belton, Missouri, an exurb of Kansas City just south of town. It was a typical trailer park and hers was a single-wide towards the end of her lot. It was white and small and had Christmas lights above the awning. That was appropriate at the moment because it was November. However, Damien said she kept them up year-round, and, for some reason, that made me smile. I loved Christmas lights and often wondered why they were only up during the holiday season.

I knocked on the door and she answered it. She was a skinny woman, probably didn't weigh more than 110 pounds, even though she was about five foot six. She had dark hair, green eyes and olive skin, just like Damien. She was weathered - she had crow's feet around her eyes and her skin looked like leather. When I got close to her, I knew why she looked like that. She reeked of cigarette smoke.

"Well, lady," she said. "Don't just stand out there looking like a lost child. Come on in."

I walked in and saw she had furniture that looked to be from the free section on Craigslist. There were pleather couches with large holes she didn't even try to sew. She had a battered coffee table in front of one of the couches and on this table was a bong. Instead of a dining room table, she had a small card table with metal legs and one chair that went with it. Her trailer didn't even have a bedroom so there was a bed tucked away in the corner. The bed looked like it had never been made, for the sheets and the comforter were strewn all over the place. Her kitchen was tiny and she didn't even have a dishwasher, so her dishes were piled up in the sink. There were a couple of cats running around.

"Have a seat. Welcome to Château Olivia." She chuckled. "This ain't Buckingham Palace, that's for sure. But why the hell do I care? I ain't no muckety-muck and never will be. Even if I won the lottery, I would never be a muckety-muck."

I nodded. I found her amusing. I was a little surprised that Damien had such an upbringing, but I shouldn't have been. After all, he told me about his mother and what she was like. It wouldn't be the first time a kid was completely different from his parents.

I took a seat on a threadbare couch and Olivia brought me a glass of water. "Would you like a Bloody Mary?" she asked me.

I shook my head. "No. That's all right."

"Oh I see, you're too good for a Bloody Mary?" Then she laughed. "I'm just busting you. I know you don't drink on the job, right?" She shook her head. "I guess that's a good thing, considering you're working on my son's case. I guess you probably shouldn't get hammered while you're questioning witnesses."

I smiled. "Yes. That's very true." I didn't tell her I was a recovering alcoholic. That was not something I usually advertised to people, especially people I just met.

"Well, you're here. Ask what you got to ask me. Don't worry, I got nothing to hide."

I had a list of notes and questions I wanted to ask her. But I wasn't quite sure what I wanted to actually get at. I just needed to talk to her and see what she knew and just let the conversation go wherever it needed to go.

"I wanted to ask you about Damien's relationship with his father. Now, from what I understand, Damien had no interest in meeting Josh. Is that right?"

"Yeah, that's right. I mean the bastard raped me and that was how Damien came into the world. Damien wanted nothing to do with him."

"Yet he established a relationship with him. Now, how did that happen? Why did you go to his father to try to get the two of them together?" I narrowed my eyes. I had the feeling Olivia might have set her own son up. Tom gave me that idea, but I didn't know why she would do that. It didn't make much sense to me, so I would have to try to satisfy myself that it didn't happen that way.

"Well, the cat was out of the bag. Damien somehow knew about his father and what he did to me, and all this time I always told him I didn't know who his father was. That was a lie, of course. I didn't want him to know his father was a rapist. And I certainly didn't want him to know his father was a muckety-muck, which is exactly what Josh Roland was. He was the king of the muckety-mucks. Man, I see what happens with those billionaire families. I see how messed up their kids end up getting. I didn't want that to happen to Damien, and that's why I never wanted him to know who his father was."

"How did he end up finding out who his father was?"

Olivia shrugged. "Hell if I know. All I know is he shows up at my door one day. Just out of the blue, he shows up. And he shows up specifically asking me about who his father was. I don't know how, but he knew something. He pestered me and I told him. I figured he would find out sooner or later. He's snoopy like that. He's one of those guys like a dog after a bone. Once something gets stuck in his craw, he doesn't let it go. So I figured I'll tell him who his dad is. What could it hurt?"

"Okay, so you told him who his father was. Did Damien try to seek him out at all? Did he call him? Do anything?"

"No he didn't. It was months. Months and he still hadn't contacted Josh. So I decided to tell Josh he has a son."

"And how did Josh take that?"

"How did Josh take the news he had a son? That his rape resulted in a kid?" She shook her head. "Not good. Not good at all. He threw a fit, to say the very least. He started cussing me, telling me he thought I would try to get his money and black-mail him."

"Is that all that happened? He simply accused you of telling him about Damien because you wanted to blackmail him?"

She took a deep breath. "God dammit. I need a smoke. Come on out on the porch. I'm trying not to smoke inside anymore. This whole place was starting to stink like one big cigarette. I never used to notice it before, but lately I've been cleaning out my nostrils with this Nettie pot thing. You see it on TV. You put this liquid up your nose and it clears it out. That's what I've been doing and now I can smell the cigarette smoke in my place. And it don't smell good. So come on out, I'm gonna smoke on the porch. I know, I know it's freezing out there. Colder than a witch's tit. You'll just have to suck it up, buttercup." Then she smiled.

She was right about one thing. There was no way I wanted to sit out on the porch with her. It *was* colder than a witch's tit. But, then again, if I wanted to get the story from her, I would have to do what she asked. I had a feeling there was a story there, and it was a story that Damien himself did not know.

Maybe he did know?

I realized I didn't really trust much of what Damien said about his father. After he admitted to me he had picked up the lamp and swung at him - this negated his entire story about him being nervous, which was why he supposedly touched the lamp in the first place - I knew there were going to be layers to the story. To say the very least.

"Now, before you tell me the rest of the story, I need to ask you one thing. Damien said you told him the reason why Josh contacted you was because he wanted to make amends. He was in an Alcoholic Anonymous program and was on the step where you're supposed to make amends to the people you've hurt. He also said you went to Josh and told him about Damien being born. He said you told him both of those things but he never said Josh was angry when you went to see him. And now you tell me something different."

"Yeah, I lied to him. I did. Listen, I decided that after all these years that Damien needed to know his dad. And if I told Damien the truth about his dad, that his dad is still a bastard and a son of a bitch, Damien would want nothing to do with him. So I might've told a white lie. I might've told him his father was working on himself and was a really nice guy." She shrugged. "So sue me."

"Well, the reason why I'm asking you these questions is because what you tell me might make me doubt Damien's entire story."

"Listen, if you're telling me you think my son did this, you're barking up the wrong tree. Yeah, my son has had problems in his life. Yeah, he's been in trouble a lot. Mainly when he was a kid and was mixed up with the wrong kind of people. He was running with the wrong crowd. And look at what happened to his crowd. They all ended up in the joint for 17 years. Held up a liquor store and a guy got killed." She shook her head. "That's the kinda guys he was running with."

"Those are the kind of guys he is still running with. Those are still his best friends. And for the record, I've met all those guys, and they're all good guys. They made mistakes when they were young. We all have. But they've pay their debts and hopefully they'll keep their noses clean."

"I know, I know. All I'm trying to say is that Damien was messed up when he was young. That has a lot to do with me and the bastard of a guy I married, Steven Harrington. I'll admit it, I wasn't the best mom in the whole world. I boozed too much, drugged too much, sold my body on the street. Yeah, I did all those things. I'm not proud of them."

"I know you're not. But please, tell me the rest about what happened when you saw Josh Roland and told him he had a son."

"Well, here's what happened. He not only got pissed off but he threatened me."

"What do you mean he threatened you? What did he threaten you with?"

"He threatened to wipe me off the face of the earth if I tried to come after him for money. He threatened to kill me if I told anybody about what had happened. And then he demanded a DNA test. When I told him I already did a DNA test, and that's how I found out for sure he was Damien's dad, hoo boy. That really enraged him."

"What do you mean, you did a DNA test already?"

"Exactly what I said. When he raped me, and I got pregnant, I decided to find out who did that to me. Who knocked me up. So, one day, when he came into the club, and was completely three sheets to the wind, I cut off a lock of his hair. I sent that shit to the lab and that's when I found out he was Damien's dad." She crossed her arms in front of her. "That's what I'm talking about. I told Josh what I did, and that really pissed him off."

"Okay, so that pissed him off. What did he do?"

"Oh, he was convinced I was just there to try to shake him down. I told him to cool his jets. If I wanted to shake him down, I would've done it a goddamn long time ago right? I mean, seriously. All these years, and I haven't even told him at all that Damien was his? I mean, Damien is 35 years old. 35 years and I haven't said a word to anybody about it. Now he suddenly thinks I'm going to try to come after him for money? I'm going to tell the media about what happened?" She shook her head. "Pretty fucking ridiculous, if you ask me."

I narrowed my eyes. "Okay, I have to ask you this question. Did you happen to get a visit from somebody by the name of Tasha Bennington? After you went to see Josh, did someone by that name come and see you?"

"Hey, how'd you know about that? Yes, I got a visit from someone named Tasha Bennington. She came over here and threatened me too."

"How did she threaten you? What did she say to you?"

"Oh, there wasn't a whole lot she could really threaten me with. I mean, look around. I ain't got a lot to lose, do I?" She shook her head. "No, I ain't got nothing to lose. And I think she knew that."

"But she threatened you anyway, right?"

"Right. She's all coming over here and telling me she'll plant shit on me and call the cops. I told her to go ahead and try. And she said I didn't want to try her." Olivia shrugged. "So, that was that."

"Yet, you did tell somebody about Josh. Your son, Damien."

"Yeah, I told him. Nobody tells me what to do. But nobody. So, after that woman Tasha came over here, I decided to tell Damien to get in contact with his dad. I would show her I can't be intimidated. Someone tries to threaten me and tell me I can't do something, it makes me want to do it even more. Let me tell you, I wasn't going to tell Damien to see his father until his father acted like that to me and that damn Tasha came over here and threatened me. After all that, I would make goddamned sure Josh knew that Damien knew about him."

"And yet you lied to Damien about his father, right?"

"Damned right I lied. What do you think would happen if I told him the truth? I'll tell you what would've happened - he would've wanted nothing to do with his dad. So I told him his dad was being all nicey-nice and he wanted to meet him."

"Olivia, you set him up."

Olivia sighed. "I know I did. And I really shouldn't have. But goddammit, I really wanted Damien to torment that old bastard. I wanted Josh to twist in the wind."

"Olivia, why do you hate Damien?" I asked that question because I was becoming irritated. This woman set Damien up. That much was inescapable. I also wanted to see what her reaction would be when I asked her that question. I wanted to read her body language and facial expressions to see if she actually *did* hate Damien.

"I don't hate Damien. What makes you think that?"

"Because you used him to get back at Josh Roland. And now Josh is dead. And there's a good possibility Damien did it." I shook my head. "I hope you're happy."

"Listen lady, my son didn't do that. He didn't kill that man."

"Olivia, you knew Josh was dangerous. You knew he's a sociopath. And he has sexual problems, to say the very least. He raped you, and from what I understand, you weren't the only one. He has treated women like dirt his entire life, from what I hear, and apparently also has a thing for very young girls." I took a deep breath. I was so angry with this woman for putting Damien in that situation.

"What you mean by that? What do you mean, he has a thing for young girls?"

"You're surprised? You're surprised that Josh would do something like molest Amelia when he came over to Damien's house for dinner?"

"Yes, I'm surprised about that. I knew the guy was a bastard, but I didn't think he was that much of a bastard."

"Well, he is. He is and he did that."

Olivia looked genuinely upset when I said that to her. "Well, if you're wondering if I regret doing what I did, the answer to that is yes. I do regret that. I should've told Damien the truth and he could have gone to see Josh with open eyes. But who am I kidding? If I would've told Damien the truth, he probably would not have gone to see him at all."

"And that would've been so bad?"

She sighed. "Twenty-twenty hindsight. Right?"

"Something like that, I guess. But there is one thing that surprises me."

"And what's that?"

"The thing that surprises me is that Josh would've been willing to go to Damien's house at all for dinner."

"Well, that's an easy one. Josh obviously thought Damien was still married to Sarah."

"And what's that supposed to mean?"

"That means that Josh was obsessed with that woman. That's what that means."

I took a deep breath. "What are you trying to say? I know Josh knew Sarah because apparently she worked for him one summer. And the reason why she worked for him was because she was acting like a spy on your behalf. She wanted to see what kind of person he was."

"Yeah, you're right about that."

"And, by the way, did Damien ever know you and Sarah were talking? Were you doing that behind his back too?"

"I wasn't doing nothing behind his back. Can't a woman have friends?"

"Yeah, I guess. But I don't quite understand why you and Sarah became friends. I don't quite understand why it was a secret from Damien as well. You're going to have to fill me in on that one."

"Listen, I had more in common with Sarah than I ever did with Damien. Me and her were like two birds of a feather."

"Do you mean you two were birds of a feather because you're both so manipulative?"

Olivia snorted and shook her head. "No, that's not what I mean. Goddammit, I told you to stop judging me. Yet, here you are, still judging me."

"Alright, alright, I'll stop judging you. Now tell me why you were talking with Sarah behind Damien's back?"

"I wanted Sarah to spy for me at Josh's company. I knew she was just the kind of girl he would hire in a second. Tall, thin, blonde, big cans, a real knockout."

"And why did you want her to spy on Josh, exactly?"

"Because I wanted her to find out what Josh was like these days. Because, believe it or not, there was a period of time when I would go ahead and tell Damien about who his father was, a period of time before he asked me about Josh. And I wanted Sarah to go over and work for him and see what kind of person he was, so I could see if I wanted Damien to talk with him."

My head was spinning. This woman was so contradictory. I didn't know which way to turn. First, she was telling me she set Damien up after knowing that Josh was a bastard. And now she was telling me she was concerned that Josh might've been a bastard, and if he was a bastard, she didn't want Damien to know about him. So either she was concerned about Damien's feelings or she wasn't. I had a feeling she sent Sarah over to spy on Josh for a reason other than the one she was telling me about.

"Olivia, I don't believe you. I don't believe you wanted Sarah to spy on Josh just because you wanted to see if Josh was a good guy or not. You knew he wasn't. He raped you all those years ago." I shuddered as I thought about my own rape. All these years later, and I still wanted revenge on Michael Reynolds. And I got it. I got my revenge on him. I knew how Olivia felt. There was no way she would've ever thought that Josh was a decent person. No, there had to be some other reason why she had Sarah spying on him.

"You tell me I'm lying?" Olivia demanded.

"Yes, I know you're lying. Now, tell me the truth as to why you wanted Sarah to spy on him. Tell me what Sarah had to gain in this whole situation. The two of you cooked something up. That much I know."

"Oh, you're so sure about that, are you? You think you're so goddamned smart, do you?"

"No, I don't think I'm so smart. However, I am a criminal defense attorney and know when somebody's lying to me. And I'm absolutely sure you're lying to me right now."

"You can think what you want. All I can tell you is that Sarah worked for him one summer and she told me he started stalking her. There was something about the way she looked that really got Josh going."

"What do you mean, stalking her?"

"Sarah said he kept asking her out, but she kept turning him down. She had no desire to get involved with that guy. Believe it or not, at that time at least, Sarah was pretty devoted to Damien. That was before the whole Amelia getting sick thing happened, and that made her run away. At that time, Sarah just wanted to make Damien happy. So she told Josh she wanted nothing to do with him and he just didn't take that for an answer."

"So, what happened with that?"

"Oh, he texted her all the time, asked her out all the time, you know, that kind of thing. Then one day, he called her into his office, locked the door and tried to take her clothes off. She had some pepper spray in her pocket and sprayed him in the eyes with it. After that, she quit that job. She told me she wanted nothing to do with him. But that didn't stop him from continually trying to call and text her and things like that. In fact, she said he drove by her house a lot."

Tom said the attack happened in a limo, but whatever. An attack is an attack. I wouldn't quibble about that detail. "Okay, so you think Damien's father wanted to have dinner with him because he thought Sarah would be there? How did he know Damien and Sarah were ever married?"

"Oh, he came over here one day to threaten me. He came into this house and saw that picture." She pointed to a picture on her bookshelf of Damien, Sarah, and the two kids. "He saw that picture, and zeroed in on it."

"Now I understand. Now I totally understand."

"What? What do you understand?"

"It confused me that he would have been so nice to Damien, considering all you've told me about how he's threatened you and how you were never to tell Damien about him. Or anybody else about him. But it makes sense he would kiss up to Damien. He thought he could get close to Sarah.

Thinking that if he could have dinner at Damien's house, he could see Sarah." I nodded. "Now it totally makes sense."

"I'm glad it makes sense to you, 'cause it sure don't make sense to me."

"Hmmm... Okay, so Josh was obsessed with Sarah. Do you know why he was so obsessed with her?"

"No, I don't know. Sarah's a beautiful woman, don't get me wrong, but I don't know why he was so stalky with her. She almost wanted to get a restraining order against him. That's how weird he was getting."

The wheels started turning in my mind. Sarah...

"Now how did Sarah react to Josh stalking her like that?"

"He creeped her out, of course. She got pissed off at me because I put her up to going over there and working for him."

"And now Sarah hates Damien. And she hates Josh as well." I nodded. "This is getting very interesting."

"When did I ever say she hated Josh?"

"I have a feeling there is more to the story. That's what I think. There's more to what Josh did to Sarah."

"Well, what do you think he did to Sarah?"

"I don't really know. I just think there's more to the story." My wheels started to turn faster. "Sarah was mentally unbalanced. That much was true. Damien told me about her mental issues and Tom Garrett also told me about them. Damien told me Sarah has been in a mental hospital and was suicidal after she left him. The way she was acting wasn't rational. It really wasn't rational for a woman to abandon a sick child the way she did. Especially since she did that by having an affair with somebody else." I had to wonder if there was more to Sarah and if she was the person I should be focusing on.

"Why do you think there was more to it?"

"I don't know, it's just a hunch. I need to find out more from Sarah herself."

"Well, good luck. She doesn't live in town anymore. Good luck trying to talk to her."

"Where is she living?"

"Last I heard, she moved to Chicago."

"Chicago is not that far. I can see her up there."

"Go ahead. I don't know what you hope to gain from it, though. And don't you have two little kids at home yourself? Who's going to watch them while you're gone? Damien certainly can't do it now. He has his hands full with his own two kids."

"I know. I understand that. You're right, I can't leave my kids. I have a sitter, her name is Sophia, she's been with me ever since the girls have been living with me, but I can't leave them."

Of course, I didn't want to tell Olivia that Abby was currently staying at the rehab facility. I went to see her at the rehab facility every evening. She still hadn't really talked to me about why she was acting like that. We were in family therapy, but, so far, she had given me nothing. I had no idea what was going on.

I sighed as I realized I couldn't just go to Chicago, not with Abby so fragile. Yet I had a feeling that Sarah might hold the key to this whole situation. I was increasingly thinking she was behind the murder of Josh. That would actually make sense to me. She was angry at Josh, angry at Damien and was mentally imbalanced. It was the perfect storm, really. She had reason to kill Josh and frame Damien. Two birds one stone, as they say.

"Well, what do you think, girly?"

"I'm thinking I got to go. Olivia, you helped out a lot, more than you know."

"Oh, now you're saying it. Now you're being all nicey-nice to me. Earlier you were thinking I was some kinda witch who wanted to kill Damien."

"I never said you wanted to kill Damien. I just didn't like the fact you set him up."

"You think Sarah did it don't you?"

"I don't know. I honestly don't know."

And that was the truth. But I was pointing towards her more and more.

That much was for sure.

CHAPTER 18

That night, I went to see my daughter Abby. Rina wanted to go with me, but I told her I really needed to spend some quality mother-daughter time with Abby. Rina made a fuss about it but I told her she needed to stay home with Sophia.

I did kind of want Rina to come with me. Yet I knew it was probably better she didn't.

Abby had a private room in one of the best rehabilitation facilities in Kansas City. After she got out of the hospital from her overdose, I had her checked into this place. I wanted to nip it in the bud. The last thing I wanted was to see her spiral downward the way I did for years and years. I didn't want her to have to battle an addiction her whole life. Especially not an addiction to something like this. It broke my heart, and I still had no idea why she turned to drugs.

I went to the facility and gave the private number I needed to give so I could see her. That was the way it was - you had to have a secret number and that was the only way people could get in and pay a visit to the people they loved.

I went up to her room, which was really a nice room. If

there was one thing I always hated about hospitals, it was the way they looked. So depressing. I hated the icky wall colors and the white tiled floors. I hated the way they smelled. I didn't know why hospitals had to be so depressing. I wanted to make sure Abby had a room that was not depressing. I had checked this place out before she ever came here, because I wanted to make sure this was the right place for her.

Abby's room was painted in the color she really liked – forest green. It was cozy. Her bed had an actual bedspread on it, with flowers. I gave her the bed spread from her own room because I wanted to make sure she was comfortable. Instead of the white tile that most hospitals have, this room had hardwood floors. It had a chest of drawers that was very attractive and I put little figurines on top of it. There was a flatscreen TV and she could look out the window and see birds feeding at the feeder.

It was 7 o'clock and she was already in her pajamas. She saw me come in the door and didn't really say anything to me. She just brought her blanket up above her shoulders, as if she was afraid of me. That was what her body language told me. She was afraid of me.

"Hey there, Buttercup."

"Hi Mom." She hung her head.

I sat down on the bed next to her. "I hope you can be home for Christmas. I have something special for you."

She hung her head again, but said nothing.

"Honey, I need to get through to you. I need you to talk to me. I'm sorry I didn't see what was happening until it was too late. I know I haven't been around as much as you would like for me to be, and I'm really sorry about that. I'm going to cut back on my hours. I promise you I will."

I knew what I was saying was falling on deaf ears. She was addicted to heroin. She was past the point where me offering to cut back on my hours would cure her. I knew it would help but I knew she needed much more than than that from me. And I didn't really know how to give it to her. I didn't know exactly what she needed. I didn't know why she was doing this.

"Mom, you don't have to do that. You really don't."

"I know I don't have to do that but I want to. You and Rina mean the world to me. I hope you understand that."

She shook her head and had tears in her eyes. "I'm so sorry I let you down. I'm so sorry about that."

"Honey, you could never let me down. You know, before you and Rina came into my life, my life was empty. That's what it was. Empty. I was sad and lonely. I had my job and my mom and dad and siblings, but I didn't really have anything that made me feel proud. That's what you and Rina have always done for me. You've always made me feel proud."

"How can you feel proud of me right now? After what I did?"

"Abby, of course I feel proud of you. Are you going to mess up? Of course you are. Granted, taking hard drugs like that is something serious. I don't want to tell you differently. I don't want you to think I feel that your taking hard drugs and being addicted to heroin is something I take lightly, because it's not. But, in the end, you're human, and you're going to do things, even serious things, that aren't good."

"But Mom, you couldn't possibly understand what I'm going through."

"I think I know." I paused. "When I was your age, I had a substance abuse problem as well. It was alcohol. I was drinking heavily when I was 13 years old. And I was drinking heavily up until a few years ago. In fact, it was you and Rina who convinced me to stop drinking. I knew I could never get custody of the two of you if I was still struggling with the alcohol problem. So, in a way, the two of you saved my life. No, strike that. The two of you *did* save my life. Not just in a way, but you did, period. Without the two of you, I would probably still be drinking."

"Why did you have problems like that?" Abby was looking at me with her big brown eyes. They were so sad, but yet, behind those eyes, I saw a look of hope and curiosity in them. Those were the first positive emotions I saw in her eyes since she'd been in this place. My heart soared just a little bit.

"Why did I have problems like that? Well, that's a good question. You see, all my life I've battled sadness. I didn't quite understand it either. I didn't know why I was so sad. All I knew was that I was. And it turned out it was nothing really that caused me to be sad, it was just something inside of me. You see, I have a disease. Not the disease of alcoholism, but I was diagnosed with bipolar disorder. Do you know what that is?"

Abby shook her head. "No. I don't know what that is. But I know what depression is." She nodded. "My counselor at school thinks I'm depressed."

"She does? How come she didn't call me about that?" That really made me angry. If there was something going on with my daughter, I deserved to know about it. I would have to give that counselor a piece my mind.

Abby just shrugged. "I don't know Mom. I don't know why she didn't talk to you about it. I think she wanted to call you. She said she would. I guess she just forgot." She pulled her blanket tighter around her. "I've been seeing her at school, several times a week." Then Abby looked ashamed. "Mom, I know I should've come to you. I know you're the first person I should've asked about what was going on with me. I wish I would have. I really wish I would have now."

"Buttercup, it's okay. But I want you to know you can come to me with anything. Anything at all. You have to understand one thing – whatever you're going through, I can relate. Believe it or not, I've not always been the together woman you see before you." I meant that to be a lighthearted joke, because as Abby has known, I've always been anything but together. "Abby, when I was your age, I was really an outcast. I wanted to be popular, but just didn't have it in me to be popular. And I know it's probably tough seeing your identical twin sister Rina ruling the school with her popularity. You don't say much about it, but I know it has to be tough to see that. But you have to understand one thing, and it's that people like you really end up ruling the world. Most of our famous actresses, actors, CEOs and people like that say they felt out of place in high school and junior high. And that drove them to be what they are. Even Taylor Swift was unpopular. She told an interviewer that she called all her friends one day to go to the mall, and each friend said they were busy. She saw those same friends, all together, at that same mall that day. She went there with her mother after all her friends rejected her."

Abby's eyes got wide. "Taylor Swift wasn't popular? Really?"

"Really. She told the interviewer that the kids at school thought she was weird. Look at her now."

Abby smiled and my heart soared. Abby *loved* Taylor Swift. Taylor was her idol, so knowing that Taylor once struggled with popularity really hit home with her. That much was obvious by her now glowing expression.

"I know you like to read, so maybe I'll find you a book about what famous people were like when they were younger," I said. "You'll see that most of them were not exactly the most popular people in their schools, but had something inside them that made them special. And I think you have the same thing."

"You think so, Mom?" And she looked down. "You're right, I do feel like an outcast at school." She swallowed hard. "Rina has tried to make her friends like me, but they don't. I'm just not like them. I would like to find my own clique at school, but it seems like nobody wants to accept me. I don't really understand why."

"Abby, is that why you start taking drugs? To fit in?"

She nodded and tears started to finally flow down her cheeks. "Yes, that's exactly why. There was this guy at school. He's one of those guys everybody likes. And he started to pay attention to me. I didn't quite know why. At first, I thought it was because he thought I was Rina. But no, he liked me. And he told me that if I did this drug, I would be cool. That's what he told me. And he told me that it would make me feel good. And I don't really feel good most of the time. So I tried it. And he was right – I did feel good, but not for long. But I really wanted to have that feeling again, so I kept trying it. And I guess that's why I'm here. I'm so sorry, Mom. I was stupid."

"Oh Abby, you're not stupid. You're anything but. You're a dear, sweet, sensitive, beautiful young girl. And you are very intelligent. You just have to believe in yourself a bit more." As I looked at her I realized one thing – I would have to monitor her for the rest of her life. If she could become addicted to heroin in such a short period of time, that told me she might have an addictive personality – there are some people in the world who just become addicted to anything they try. I wondered if Abby was the same.

I also felt so guilty I never even noticed the changes. I mean, I did notice the changes, but I didn't ever dream she was taking drugs. I needed to wake up. I needed to be there for her more. Rina too. If Abby was the addictive sort, Rina probably was too. Rina was much more sure of herself than Abby, but that didn't mean she was immune. I would definitely talk to her about drugs and about what she should do if anybody ever offered her something. In short, I would have to be much more diligent with both my girls. With Abby, I would have to make sure she knew I was on her side and would understand and no matter what happened, she could come to me.

"Mom, I'm concerned I'm here. I'm going to miss my final exams if I have to stay here for much longer."

"Don't worry, Abby. I've spoken with your teachers and they've all agreed you can make up the final exams whenever you get back into school. They want you to be well. So do I. So you have to stay here for as long as it takes to make sure you don't go back to what you were doing. And I'll be here every evening. I promise that."

I stayed until she fell asleep and then went home.

As I drove home, I was totally in my head. I loved that little girl so much and I was terrified something would happen and I would lose her.

If that happened I didn't know if I could ever recover.

CHAPTER 19

Sarah appeared in my office, after I threatened her with a subpoena for a deposition. I didn't actually intend to depose her, but I needed her to come to my office so I could interview her. She came willingly, because she didn't want to be deposed.

She wasn't happy about having to come and made her displeasure known.

"Okay I'm here, this better be good." Sarah was exactly as Olivia described her. She was tall, blonde and beautiful. Big blue eyes, creamy skin, didn't wear makeup because she didn't have to. She was willowy and slim but had large breasts. She was the kind of girl who made people like me, and Abby, intimidated. At least, she was the kind of girl who would've intimidated in high school. Right now, she was just another witness for me to depose. And I had power over her.

That was satisfying, in a way.

"Sit down. I have some questions I need to ask you."

"I gathered that. I have no idea why you want to see me. I don't know what this whole thing has to do with me. All I know is I'm living in Chicago now and have left my old life behind. And when I say I've left my old life behind, it means I've left my old life behind. That means I'm not interested in revisiting the past. So, as soon as you're through with me here, I'm going back to Chicago. And please don't tell Damien I was here."

I nodded, silently thinking I couldn't believe she would be the way she was. She had two kids here. Two children who thought she abandoned them, and they thought that for good reason - she *did* abandon them. If she was the kind who could do something like that to her kids, in my book, she was the kind who could do anything.

"I understand and I didn't tell Damien you were coming. So your secret is safe with me. I just need to ask you a few questions."

She cocked her head, crossed her arms and looked like she wanted to kill me. She narrowed her beautiful blue eyes and the look in those eyes was cold. Just plain cold. I usually could look into somebody's eyes and know what kind of person they were. That was always a gift I had. And I could usually see when there was very little warmth in a person. As I looked into Sarah's eyes, I realized she was not a warm person.

She was cold as ice.

"Well, let's get on with it." She looked at her watch. "I want to be done with this within two hours. I need to be back on a plane tonight. So get on with it."

I whipped out a pen and paper. "Okay, let's get started. First of all, I need to know how you came to know Josh Roland."

"I'm sure Olivia told you. She sent me over there to work for him." She bit her lower lip. "That's what happened. I wasn't working that summer, because, as you know, I'm a kindergarten teacher, and I got a job working for Josh Roland."

"What were you doing for him?"

She took a deep breath. "I was one of his assistants." She raised an eyebrow. "That's what I did."

"What kind of work did you do for him?"

"I managed his calendar, found fundraisers for him to attend, made charitable donations for him, and managed some of his financial records."

"You did." I raised an eyebrow. "What financial records were you managing?"

"I managed his investment records. What that means is he gave me the information on his investments and I input the data into the computer."

"I see. Did Olivia have you go to work for Josh because she wanted to find out information about his financial dealings? Is that what happened?"

She looked at me. I could see the wheels turning in her head. I suddenly realized that was probably what the deal was. "Why do you ask that?"

"Listen, I know how Olivia felt about him. I understand it. He raped her many years ago, and I think she probably wanted some kind of revenge upon him. That's what I think. And I think she used you to get that revenge. You were looking to see if he was doing some insider trading, weren't you? You were assigned to go there and get a job from him so you could blow the whistle. Is that right?"

"Now, why would you think that?"

"Because I don't know any other reason why Olivia would want you to do this. And what was in it for you?"

She sighed. "Listen, I know what you're getting at, and it won't work. You're trying to figure out if Olivia and I are somehow in on killing Josh Roland. Especially me. You know I have it in for Damien and you're thinking I killed Josh and pinned it on Damien. Aren't you?"

"That thought crossed my mind. But I need to find out why

you worked for him. And what kind of incentive you personally had to do it. That's what I'm trying to figure out."

"You're so sure there was some incentive for me to do it?" She narrowed her eyes. "Maybe you need to figure that out on your own."

"Maybe I will. It would be more helpful if you could tell me about it, but rest assured I will dig until I find out what you gained from working for Josh. Why you would be interested in bringing him down? I know why Olivia would want to, but why would you care? You're the one whose neck was on the line here, not Olivia. You were the one whose life probably would've been threatened by Tasha Bennington if you did what you were assigned to do. If you blew the whistle on him, you would've been a dead woman. I know people like Tasha Bennington and they will do anything, literally anything, to make sure Josh is protected. Did you know that? Did you realize Tasha Bennington probably would have had you killed, if she couldn't blackmail you, if you tried to blow the whistle on Josh?"

She shook her head. "Harper, you don't know Jack." But as I looked in her eyes, I knew that what I was telling her was a surprise. I didn't think she knew about Tasha Bennington. I had a feeling she was digging into Josh's financial records but never got the chance to actually blow the whistle on him. She quit working for him before she could find out what she needed to find out.

Josh must've done something terrible to her, something that would have caused her to abandon her mission prematurely.

"Are we done here?" Her arms were crossed and she glared at me.

"No, we're not done here. Why did you quit working for Josh?"

"I'm sure Olivia told you about that too. And don't look at me like you don't know what I'm talking about. Because I know you spoke with her, and I know she told you why I quit."

"She told me something about it, but I don't think she told me the entire story. She didn't tell me what the real reason why you quit working for him. You had a job to do and didn't do it. You quit before you could complete the job you're supposed to do. Now why would you quit early like that?"

She shrugged. "As you said, Tasha Bennington threatened me. That's why I quit early. That's why I abandoned what I was supposed to do."

She all but confirmed my initial suspicions as to why she would go to work for him. She really was working for Josh in an effort to find out enough about his financials to bring him down. But I also knew, I just had a hunch, she had no idea who Tasha Bennington was. She was just telling me Tasha forced her to quit. That wasn't the real story.

"Sarah, you're going to have to fill in the puzzle pieces here. Either you're going to do it now or when I put you under oath at trial. And trust me, if I find out what the whole story is, you will be subpoenaed for trial. And I will make you get on the stand and tell the court your involvement with Josh."

"You think I killed him? That's what you're thinking, isn't it? Admit it. You think I killed him."

"I'm not going to say one way or the other. I'm just saying you need to come clean on why you started working for him. What's in it for you, and why did you quit? Those are the three questions I need to have answered. Either you're going to answer them or I'll find someone who will."

She finally looked defeated. She knew there would be no way out. I would get the answers I sought, so she had to come clean.

"I hated that man," she said. "I hated him with the passion of a thousand suns." She looked out the window.

"Why?"

She took a deep breath and let it out.

"He was the reason my father killed himself."

CHAPTER 20

She looked at me with raised eyebrows and cocked her head. "Is that what you expected would come out of me? Is that what you're looking for?"

Now I was getting somewhere. "What do you mean, he was responsible for your father killing himself?"

"My father was a good man. A very good man. He had a construction company and contracted with Josh to build an apartment complex downtown. It was a mistake to not get his money up front, but he was just so excited to be working with a renowned billionaire such as Josh Roland. He thought he finally made it. If he did a good job for Josh, the money would roll in, because Josh would refer my dad's business to all his rich friends. My dad was so excited about working for him that he went ahead and contracted with him but didn't ask for any kind of a down payment. He didn't ask for anything from Josh. On the contract it said the payment for the apartment building was to come after the building was built."

"Okay. So what happened?"

"Well my father, his company wasn't very big. He didn't have a lot of assets in his company and not a lot of cash. I mean, he had enough cash to build the apartment complex, but didn't have much left over after that. So he spent his company's money buying the materials and hiring the men. And he did a very good job. A very good job. But by the end of it, he was tapped out."

"What happened?"

"What do you think happened? Josh refused to pay. He made some excuse about poor workmanship and that was just bullshit. It was just an excuse because he didn't want to pay his bill. My father filed a lawsuit for breach of contract, but Josh is a billionaire and my father was just a lowly construction company owner. That's all he was. He was a little guy. He didn't have enough money to pay attorneys to get to the end of the case. Josh had an army of attorneys. My father could barely afford even one. And so Josh just got away with it. The case never went to court and Josh never paid a dime. My father ended up declaring bankruptcy because of it. Josh owed him over a million dollars. My father put $200,000 into the apartment complex and that was enough to bankrupt his entire company."

I felt so sorry for Sarah's father. A little guy like that being crushed by the big guy. Josh treated her father just like he was a bug to be squashed. That made me sick. "So, your father's company went bankrupt. Because of Josh. What happened after that?"

"What do you think happened after that? My father had to find a job. He had to take care of his family. He went to work for a construction company, getting paid $15 an hour. He could barely make ends meet. He was broken by Josh Roland. Josh not only refused to pay him, but he took away his pride. I'll never forget how I came home one day and my father tried to explain to my sister and me how he couldn't afford Christmas presents for us. Then he told us we would have to move from our three-bedroom house into an apartment." She swallowed hard. "My father killed himself that Christmas Eve. Put a gun to his head and pulled the trigger."

Sarah was crying by that time and so was I. I bit my lower lip, but the tears came down my face. I felt awful for her, for her sister, her mother, but most of all for her father. A man whose livelihood was taken away by one cheating bastard.

"Well, I can understand why you would try to bring him down. But why didn't you complete the job? Why didn't you do what you were going to do? You were looking through his financial records because I think you knew you'd find irregularities."

"Oh yes, I knew I would find irregularities with him. I knew that for sure. He was just the kind of corrupt asshole in his business dealings to have all kinds of financial crimes I could find if I worked for him. And yes, you are right about one thing - I would turn him in to the authorities the second I found the evidence I was looking for."

"Did you not find any kind of evidence he was up to criminal activity?"

"No, actually I found a lot of evidence about it. I was supposed to copy as much financial information as I could on an external jump drive and give that to the authorities. That's what I was supposed to do. I never got a chance to do that."

"Why is that? Why didn't you actually have a chance to do that?"

She looked down at the table. "Something happened and I knew I could never go back to his office again. I could never see him again."

"What happened?"

"What do you think happened?" She nodded. "I think you know."

I nodded. "He raped you, didn't he?"

"Yes he did."

CHAPTER 21

Sarah told me about what Josh had done, and I understood that if she killed Josh, she had a damned good reason for doing so. The guy was responsible for her father killing himself and he raped her. If she killed him, I certainly didn't blame her.

Sarah put her hands in front of her and crossed them tightly together. "Is that what you need to know? Is this what you were seeking from me?"

"I'm very sorry about what happened to you. I am very sorry for what Josh took from you."

"You don't know the half of it." She bit her lower lip. She blinked. "After he raped me, he threatened my life. He told me if I ever said a word to anybody, I would be dead."

"Okay, and –"

"And then I was pregnant. I was pregnant and didn't know who was the father." She took a deep breath. "I didn't know who was the father. So I got an abortion." Then she scoffed. "I got an abortion. It could very well have been Damien's child. I didn't know. I certainly wouldn't take that chance. I certainly wouldn't bring a child into the world who possibly had Josh's genes. And could you imagine? Josh would've been my child's father, possibly, and also my child's grandfather. How sick is that? How sick would that have been?"

"And you knew at this time that Josh was Damien's father, correct?"

"Of course I knew this. Olivia told me he was. I thought that was pretty ironic. The man who ruined my life by killing my father was my father-in-law."

"And you never told Damien Josh was his dad, correct?"

"Of course I never told Damien."

"Did you ever get any kind of indication that Damien knew who his father was all these years? Until recently that is."

"No."

"I just needed to check."

"I was going to tell Damien. After he kicked me out of the house, I was going to tell him who his father was. I was going to rub it in his face. But I realized I would tell Damien for the wrong reasons so I decided to keep my mouth shut. I still don't know how Damien found out about it. Olivia said he just pressed her one day on who his father was and she finally had to come clean."

I put my hand on her shoulder. "That must've been devastating for you. What he did to you, that's unforgivable."

"Yes it was. But I know you think I killed him. I didn't. Trust me on this, I didn't kill him. Did I want to kill him? You goddamned right I did. I wanted to kill him after he did what he did to my father. I was only 10 years old at the time. But I would never forgive him for that. Ever. My father was a thriving businessman. He was doing very well for himself. And then Josh broke him. He broke him. Single-handedly. You don't forgive something like that."

"No, I guess you probably wouldn't."

"You're right. And I didn't forgive him. But I didn't kill him. I didn't kill him."

I made notes and looked up at her. I would have to ask another question, and I really didn't want to. But I had to.

"Sarah, Damien told me you were in a mental hospital. After the first time you and Damien broke up, he said you were in a mental hospital after trying to commit suicide. Tell me about that."

"How is any of that your business?" She crossed her arms in front of her. "I'd like to know how you made that your business?"

"Well, it's pretty simple, really. You're right, I am looking at you for Josh's murder. I won't lie."

"Oh okay. You're thinking I'm a crazy bitch, and the fact I was in a mental institution proves it, is that right? Because a crazy bitch would kill Josh and frame her ex-husband. I understand that." Then she shook her head. "For your information, I was in the mental hospital because I tried to commit suicide, just like Damien told you. That was the only reason why. I was depressed. I'm not crazy, I'm just depressed."

I had to understand that. I, too, was in a mental hospital, for a week, because I was having a manic episode. This was before I knew I was bipolar. All my life I thought I was just depressed, when in actuality, I had bipolar disorder. I certainly couldn't press her about her stay in a mental institution and I certainly couldn't, in good conscience, use that against her. God forbid somebody used my mental illness against me.

"I do understand that. More than you know. I just had to ask the question."

"Well, now you have your answer. I'm not a sociopath, I'm not a psychopath, I'm not delusional, I'm not schizophrenic. I just fought depression my whole life. Ever since my father killed himself, I've been depressed off and on. My brother died when I was young, too. He was only 14 and I was 10. Yes, I lost him just a few months after I lost my father. I always blamed Josh for my brother Noah's death as well. It was the stress of losing our father, I think, that killed him. He was battling cancer for two years. He was getting better, but after my father died, he just went downhill. So I lose my father, and a few months later, my brother dies. And it's just my mother, my sister and me, all of a sudden. I mean, two years before all that, there were five of us living in the house, happy together. Our lives were charmed. We had it all. Sunday drives into the country, game nights, movie nights, camping, going to the beach, family trips. The whole nine. And then, just like that, my brother gets sick, my father dies, my brother dies. My mother, she was so devastated by losing both her son and her husband that she was never the same. So yes, I started to become depressed. Anybody would, if they had the kind of life I had."

I realized that. "Okay, I'm very sorry to hear about everything that happened to you. I honestly am. What you went through when you were a young girl was far beyond what anybody should've gone through. And I really don't blame you for hating Josh."

"I did hate him. But I didn't kill him. You have to believe me about this."

I didn't say anything. I did not believe her. I didn't necessarily disbelieve her, but I certainly didn't believe her. I didn't know the truth.

What I did know was that if Sarah killed him, I really didn't blame her.

CHAPTER 22

That Monday, I needed to go to Damien's arraignment. In Jackson County, the defendant is arraigned after the case goes to the grand jury. The grand jury is who decides if the case goes forward or if it's dismissed. In cases like murder cases, you don't get what is called a preliminary hearing. A preliminary hearing is basically an evidentiary hearing where the prosecutor puts his or her evidence on and the judge decides if there's enough evidence to formally charge the accused. In a preliminary hearing, opposing counsel is allowed to be there and question witnesses and try to poke holes in the prosecutor's case. However, when it comes to grand juries, neither the defendant nor the defendant's attorney are allowed to be present. In fact, neither the defendant nor the defendant's attorney even know when it happens. Grand juries convene in secret and render their judgment in secret as well. I never thought that was a fair process, but it was what it was.

And, of course, Damien's case went to the grand jury and they decided there was enough evidence for the case to go forward. That was called a True Bill, which meant Damien was indicted. So Damien had an arraignment in the division that arraigned most of the cases of Jackson County. That judge, whose name was Judge Hewitt, would then assign the case to a trial division. After the case was assigned to the trial division, I would also find out who the opposing counsel would be.

I hoped the prosecutor would not only be fair but hopefully wouldn't have it in for Damien for one reason or another. Damien being a defense counsel, I knew he probably ruffled the feathers of quite a few people in the prosecutor's office. I personally hoped the person trying the case would be Allie Hughes. I knew she had a crush on him and I knew the two of them had gone out a few times. Damien and Allie were not currently dating, mainly because he couldn't really date anybody. He couldn't leave the house except to go to his job. Yet I knew the two of them liked one another, so I knew Allie would be very fair. As long as Damien didn't piss her off for some reason, of course.

I picked up Damien for his arraignment. He looked better than the last time I saw him. He was clean-shaven and looked like he had a bit of hope. The last time I saw him, he looked very downtrodden. Very defeated. But today, his body language was different. He had a smile on his face and his posture was straighter. He looked me right in the eye.

"I look forward to this," he said with a smile.

"You do? Why are you looking forward to your arraignment?"

"Because I think it's time to get on with it. I was sitting in this house moping for this long. It's time for me to get my fighting spirit back. I've been feeling sorry for myself all this time. And I can't wait to see who we're going to get for a judge."

"That's the spirit! That's what I want to hear from you. I want to hear that you know we'll beat this case. And I think we are."

"Do you have any idea who might have done this?"

I shook my head. "I don't know. I have my hunches, but I really don't know."

"Who do you think might have done it?"

"Right now, I'll admit it. I'm looking at both your mom and ex-wife."

He sighed. "I don't blame you for looking at Sarah for this. She hates me. She could frame me for murder without even thinking about it. I don't know why she would want to kill Josh, but I know why she would want to kill somebody and make it look like I did it."

"I guess you don't know." I nodded. "Of course you don't know. Sarah never confided in you."

"What do you mean? What would she have confided in me?"

"She hated Josh." And I told him the story. I told him what Sarah told me about how Josh was responsible for her father killing himself. However, I didn't tell him the other part – that Josh raped her and she had an abortion. I thought that would devastate him. Damien would have to know there was a 50/50 chance the child she aborted was his. I didn't want to add insult to injury. If it came to it, of course, I would have to tell him. If I would seriously pursue her as an alternative suspect in the murder, I would have to tell him everything. But at the moment, I thought it better he didn't know that part.

Damien nodded. "That makes sense. I knew Sarah's father had killed himself, but she never really told me much about it. She certainly never told me about how he lost his business, and that was why he killed himself." He shook his head. "But that bastard, Josh. That bastard. How could he do something like that? How could somebody worth billions do something like that to a little guy? I don't know who killed him, but whoever did it did the world a favor. Sociopaths like him deserve it."

I had to agree with that. "Anyhow, Sarah had reason to kill him. And since she has it in for you as well, it would make sense that maybe she did it."

Damien looked out the window. "I know what you're saying, Harper. I know why you think Sarah did it. I think she might have. But I don't want to believe that about her. I was married to the woman. I loved her. It pains me to think the mother of my children might have to go to prison for the rest of her life. Nate's already very angry with me because he blames me for Sarah leaving. If she has to go to prison for killing my father, I don't know if Nate would ever recover."

"What about Amelia? How would she feel if Sarah went to prison?"

Damien shrugged. "Amelia is taking the divorce much better than Nate ever has. Amelia is not that close with her mother and hasn't been for quite a while. You have to remember, Sarah left us and abandoned Amelia when she was very sick. Amelia has no affection for her. If something happened and her mother went prison, I don't think she'll be unaffected. It'll no doubt be psychologically damaging. But I think she'll take it better than Nate would." Damien shook his head. "If something like that happened and the kids' mother went to prison, it would be extremely damaging for both of them. So I pray she wasn't behind this."

I put my hand on Damien's shoulder as I drove along. "Well, that's just a theory I have. Tom Garrett is still on the case. He's still doing his investigation. I'm going to see him in a couple of days. Hopefully he'll have something for me. Some more evidence as to who might have done this. Right now, though, Sarah is looking pretty good to me. I'm sorry to say that."

"That's okay. You're just doing your job. But my mother, you said you suspected her as well. Why do you suspect her?"

"Damien, I don't think you know how angry your mother is with you."

"Oh yes I do. I know she is very angry with me. But things have been getting better."

"They might be getting better, but –"

"But what?"

I shook my head. "I still think there's a possibility your mother is behind this. I need to rule her out. I know why she would want to kill Josh - after all, he raped her all those years ago. She really had it in for him. Remember, she put Sarah up to working for Josh in an effort to find damaging information to send him to prison. And, I'm sorry to say, but after meeting her, I would not put it past her to frame you for killing your father. That's all I'm saying."

I looked over at Damien and could tell my words were really affecting him. He had his thumb and forefinger gripping the top of his nose and his eyes were screwed shut. He looked like he was trying to stop himself from crying. He shook his head. "Oh God, Harper. I knew my mother was angry with me. I just didn't think she would do something like this. I didn't think she was angry enough to want to see me behind bars."

"I'm not saying she is. I'm just saying I don't want to rule her out just yet. Listen, Damien, as I said, Tom is doing his investigation, and I think that when he does his investigation, there will a lot of other suspects coming out of the woodwork. Josh Roland, your father, was a bastard. He hurt a lot of people. I'll be looking at a lot of people for his murder."

"Okay. But you have to narrow it down. You have to figure out one thing – who not only wanted Josh dead but also wanted me to take the fall."

"Right. That's the reason I'm looking at your ex-wife and mother so hard. They seem to have reasons to be angry with both you and your father. But I'm sure there's somebody else out there. I'm sure there is."

"I still think you need to look at the governor." Damien bit his bottom lip. "He had the most reason to be angry with me and certainly could've arranged for me to take the fall."

I nodded. I still thought that was a long shot. Granted, the governor certainly had it in for Damien. But why would he have killed Josh? That was a question in my head. That was one thing I got stuck on as I'd inquired with Tom about it several times. And, thus far, I could not find anything that would make the governor want to kill Josh. In fact, it was just the opposite. The governor got millions of dollars in campaign money from Josh and companies associated with him. If the governor killed Josh, he would be killing the goose that laid the golden egg. I just couldn't imagine he'd do something like that.

"At any rate, I have a motion to inspect the crime scene," I said. "I'll be looking specifically for any kind of surveillance equipment. That's the only thing that would make sense to me. You told me you swung the lamp at Josh and he was killed by that same lamp. Somebody had to have been surveying Josh's office for them to know that he or she should kill him with that lamp. If somebody is framing you, they had to know you were brandishing the lamp earlier. Otherwise it's just too much of a coincidence."

"You don't think the governor did it, do you?" Damien seemed disappointed by this.

"At the moment, no I don't. The governor and Josh had a business arrangement from what I could understand. Josh obviously wanted favorable legislation for his business, so he gave quite a lot of money to the governor. I just don't see the governor shutting down that gravy train. That's the only thing."

We got to the courthouse and took the elevator to the second floor, which was where Judge Hewitt, the arraignment judge, presided. We went in the courtroom, and, as usual, all the attorneys were gawking their heads at Damien. I heard them whispering and gave them a dirty look. I would have to shut down the gossiping. They had no right to be talking behind Damien's back. I heard the whispers, I knew what they were saying, and it was bullshit.

"Hello there, counselor," Judge Hewitt said to me as I walked in the door. "You're first on the docket, so come on up."

I went up there. Instead of the opposing counsel, it was usually one prosecutor doing all the arraignments. In this case, the prosecutor was Byron Wicker.

The judge read the charges to Damien, and Damien entered a plea of not guilty.

"Counselor, do you have any motions you need me to take up at the moment?"

"Yes, Your Honor. I do have a Motion to Inspect the Crime Scene on file."

Judge Hewitt looked at the file in front of him and nodded. "Mr. Wicker, do you have any objections to this fine lady inspecting the crime scene?"

"No, Your Honor."

"Okay then, the motion to inspect the crime scene is granted. Your case will be assigned to Division 47." And then he called the next case.

Division 47. That was a good one. The Judge in Division 47 was named Gina Grant. She was somebody who came from the Public Defender's office and I'd worked with her. I always had got along with her, too. She was about 50 years old and very attractive. She kept herself in shape – she was a runner and also did a lot of biking. She looked much younger than her years. She was funny, sarcastic and sharp as hell. And, above all, she was a fair judge.

"We drew a good one. I like Gina a lot." I felt a little bit more relaxed when I found out Gina would be our judge. She was a defense attorney. A lot of times, the Circuit Judges came from the prosecutor's office. It was nice to get one from the defense bar.

Damien nodded his head. "I agree. I've had cases in front of her myself, and have always been impressed with her. It definitely could've been worse."

"For sure. Now I wonder what prosecutor will be trying the case."

Damien smiled. "I hope it's Allie."

"What's going on with her? Between you and her?"

"Well, we've been talking. She's been calling and emailing me. She's very worried about me. I really want to go out with her, but not until after this is done. This has taken up almost all my mental energy. There's very little I can think about except for this."

"That's understandable. Well, we're through with that part. I'll go to the crime scene tomorrow and have it thoroughly inspected. If I can find surveillance equipment, the only other question I'll have is who installed it. From there, I think we can figure it out."

I drove Damien home and he invited me in.

"Sure, I'll come in for a little while. I have to get to the rehab center though. Abby's still in there."

"That's such a shame. I'm so sorry to hear that about Abby. Do you understand her? Do you know why she would use?"

"I do. I do understand it. And it worries me. It's always kind of worried me that the girls are in such a high-dollar school. I never really wanted them to be around a bunch of rich kids, because I always had the impression that rich kids have a lot of money and could spend that money on things like drugs. But at the same time, I know the school they're going to is the best in town. And they get the best education there. So it's a trade-off. I don't feel comfortable with them being around kids from very wealthy families, but I certainly like the education they get there. Now Abby apparently has fallen prey to the fast lane. I'll have to constantly monitor her when she gets out of the rehab facility, to make sure she's not backsliding. The last thing I want is to have her battle substance abuse addiction, like I have my entire adult life."

"Give her my regards."

"Oh, I will. She really likes you. And she's very concerned about you."

"I'm concerned about me too, but I know things will turn out okay. And I'm very concerned about her as well. I care about her very much and wish I could be there for her too. I know what you're going through in a way. My daughter was sick for a long time, and it took a lot out of me. A lot. She's okay now, knock on wood. So, Harper, if there's anything I can do for you, you just let me know."

"I will. But at the moment, it's just something I have to deal with on my own. And Axel, of course, has been with me, every step of the way. He told me about Abby in the first place. I really wish I was more in tune with Abby and had seen the signs myself, but I didn't. I'm ashamed to say I didn't. But Axel did. Axel knew before I ever did. He's been so great."

"You're lucky. You're lucky to have a good guy like that on your side."

"I know I am." And I really did consider myself lucky. Even though Axel did a very shady thing, it didn't define who he was. That was important – he wasn't defined by the fact he stole from the police department to keep his brother out of prison. He was a good guy who did a desperate, stupid thing. None of us were perfect and I had to always remind myself of that fact.

I stayed and talked with Nate and Amelia for a couple of hours, with Damien around. And then, after that, I had to beg off because I had to see my own daughter. I was missing her, and that night, I had promised Rina she could go and see Abby. Rina was very excited about that, because she was missing her sister as well.

I finally left Damien's house, feeling out of sorts. There was something nagging at me. I didn't quite know what it was, but it was like a rock in my shoe. I just couldn't get rid of it.

Maybe I could figure out what that rock was when I saw the crime scene.

CHAPTER 23

The next day I went to Josh's office. It was cordoned off by yellow tape crisscrossing the door. I stepped around the yellow tape and saw the scene as the officers must've seen it. Of course, the lamp that was used as the murder weapon was not in the office, but everything else apparently was undisturbed. I had an officer with me and also had on a pair of plastic gloves. I had a feeling that what I was looking for was in this room somewhere. I decided to figure out where.

Josh's office was enormous. Ceilings were a good 20 feet high, and one of his walls was a glass one that looked out upon the city. He evidently had a taste for fine art. There were paintings on the wall that were probably worth hundreds of thousands of dollars, if not millions. He also had a taste that veered slightly towards the Orient. The rug beneath his desk, the silk scrolls on the wall, the bonsai tree on a glass table next to his couch, various vases, and a Buddha statue next to a fountain, were all indications he had a taste for the Far East.

That was when I remembered he'd actually been to China, Japan and Taiwan several times. On his business travels.

I walked around the office looking at everything. There are a lot of crevices to look at. I looked behind every painting. I picked up every statue, paperweight and lamp I could see, looking for some kind of surveillance equipment. I had a professional with trained to find bugs. His name was Robert Lightner. He, too, had on a pair of rubber gloves. He walked slowly around the room, looking at every single crevice and space.

"What are you looking for Harper?" Officer Matt Johnson, the officer who was with me, asked.

"Did anybody happen to sweep this office for bugs or surveillance equipment?"

"Yes, I believe they did. And nothing was found. Why do you ask that question?"

I shook my head. "I just wondered, that's all."

There wasn't much this crime scene could really tell me, considering I couldn't find any kind of surveillance equipment. The only thing I gleaned from this was that Josh Roland was apparently somebody who liked art from the Far East. What that told me, I didn't know.

I looked over at Robert, after about an hour of inspecting the scene, and he shook his head. "Nothing here, although I can tell something was here." He pointed to the wall. "There, behind that Chinese silk scroll. There was some equipment back there but it looks like it's been gone for some time. Maybe removed better than six months ago."

My ears perked up at that, but it didn't really help me. Not if the surveillance equipment had been gone for so long. The next thing, of course, I would have to inspect the lamp itself. Maybe that could give me some answers.

Maybe. But in this case, answers were hard to come by.

CHAPTER 24

"Okay Tom, what you have you got for me?" I asked. I was in my office and Tom was sitting across from me with his research in his lap. Damien couldn't make the meeting, even though he was scheduled to, as he had an emergency hearing in Platte County, which was the county just north of Kansas City.

"I think I found some interesting tidbits of information you need to know," he said.

"That goes without saying, but go ahead and let me know what you found out," I said.

"Do you remember what you were talking about, when you said there had to be some kind of surveillance equipment in that office?"

My ears perked up. "Yes. I know what you're saying. But I went to the office and didn't find anything. And I asked the officer who came with me. He said they had already swept the office for surveillance equipment. That was one of the first things I did. So that seems to be a dead-end. Robert Lightner, my expert, said there had been equipment in that office, but it had been gone for some time."

"I don't think it was a dead end."

"What are you talking about?"

"I found out some interesting things about the governor. You know how you always assumed Josh Roland and the governor were on good terms? You always assumed that because Josh Roland was continually giving money to the governor?"

"Yeah. That's what I've always assumed. Why do you ask that question?"

"Well, it's not as cut and dried as all that. Listen, it turns out Josh Roland might've had reason to blackmail the governor. And the one thing I found, is that, as of late, Josh Roland has not given the governor a dime in campaign contributions. Yet it seems there has been a lot of favorable executive orders that have come out of the governor's office, executive orders that directly benefit Josh's company and directly hurt his competitors. And this was just within the past year."

"What do you mean? What kind of executive orders did he issue that benefited Josh and hurt his competitors?"

"Well, as you know, Josh's company is biotech. Aragon International. Governor Weston has the ability to make executive orders that affect companies within his state. He issued an Executive Order to a regulatory agency that adversely affected Aragon's closest competitor in the state. Aragon and the competitor, whose name is Lysis International, both are focused in the field of crop technology. They both focused on finding ways to genetically modify crops so they're more resistant to diseases and parasites. There's been a race between the two companies to find the perfect crop – the kind of crop that farmers can harvest without having to worry about spraying it for bugs. The kind of hearty crop that would be valuable to the state."

"Yes, I'm aware of what his firm does. I also am aware the

firm is involved in developing drugs as well. But what kind of executive order did you find that hurt Lysis and helped Aragon?"

Well, Lysis was using a particular kind of genetic modification that was outlawed by executive fiat. It was a regulation that Governor Weston imposed upon the biotech industries in the state. It just so happened that this particular regulation all but crippled Lysis, which gave a big boost to Aragon's bottom line. The technology was being used by Lysis, but not Aragon."

"What kind of technology was that?"

"It's a certain kind of recombinant DNA modification that Lysis had developed. They were seeking a patent on this particular technique they were using, it was so novel. Now, I know the next question you'll ask me is whether the governor was justified in outlawing it." Tom shook his head. "I've looked over the research articles on this kind of technology, and, thus far, it seems to be completely safe. There's a ton of scientific articles about it and it doesn't seem to be any worse for the environment than any other kind of recombinant DNA technique. So, it seems as though the governor outlawed this particular technique specifically to hurt Aragon's largest competitor."

I tapped my fingers on the table as I listened to him. "Now that's interesting to me. I mean, you said Josh had stopped giving money to the governor, recently, yet he got the favorable executive order after he stopped giving to him. Is that what you're saying?"

"Yes, that's exactly what I'm saying."

"Did you happen to find out why that would be?"

"I did." Tom nodded his head. "I found out what Josh possibly had over the governor."

"What was that?"

"Well, I found out that one of the senators in the state is actually planning to retire. Sen. John Cantor is the senior senator from the state of Missouri, and he has not announced it yet, but he plans on retiring before the next election. He is stepping down because of his health. What that means, of course, is the governor will have to appoint somebody in his place."

"Okay. And?" This was intriguing to me. I kind of knew where this was going and hoped I was right.

"Well, I found out the governor has been trying to sell the seat to the highest bidder. He's actually been trying to offer the senator's seat to different candidates, in exchange for campaign contributions."

I nodded. "That's the kind of thing that got the governor of Illinois, Rod Blagojevich, convicted of a felony, and he was sentenced to 14 years in prison. He was pardoned by Trump, but if he wasn't, he would still be serving time. That's exactly what Blagojevich did to land in prison. Well, that and a lot of other corruption charges, but that was the main one."

"Exactly. And here's the thing. Josh apparently was one of the people the governor made that offer to. And, from what I understand, Josh was planning on turning the governor over to the authorities for doing that. At least, that's what he threatened the governor with. What actually happened is that he threatened the governor with turning this information over to the authorities, but if the governor offered him favorable executive orders and regulations that helped his company, he would look the other way. In other words, Josh was blackmailing the governor."

Josh was blackmailing the governor. "How did Josh obtain the proof he needed to turn the governor over to the authorities?"

Tom smiled. "The governor went to see him in his office and didn't know Josh had surveillance equipment in there."

"Interesting. When did he have it installed?"

"He had it installed in his office about 10 years ago. Josh

Roland was apparently a very paranoid person. He has a reason to be, of course. People really had it in for him. So, he had surveillance equipment installed, equipment that only he knew about. It's pretty obvious that if the women he harassed in that office knew he had surveillance equipment in there, they would try to use that against him. But only he had access to it."

"Still, even if he was the only one who had access to it, anybody suing him could have those tapes subpoenaed. He was taking a big risk by doing that."

"Yes, he was definitely taking a risk. I suppose he figured that it was a risk he was willing to take, however, because if anybody ever threatened him in his office, he would have the evidence against them. And, as I said, only he knew about it, so the women who sued him didn't know to subpoena it. It was a secret. But it certainly came in handy with the governor. Josh had the governor on video offering to sell the Senate seat to him. And then Josh used that as leverage against Governor Weston. Because of that, the governor was willing to do anything at all for Josh. If Josh said jump, the governor said how 'how high?' That's how it was."

"Hmmmmm.... So, I wonder why Josh chose to take that equipment out. That's an interesting wrinkle in the case."

"Well, here's what I found out. Josh's surveillance equipment was hacked into so he had it removed. He was afraid somebody could access it and use it against him."

"Do you know who might've hacked into him?" I asked.

"No. I just found out he was hacked but I didn't find out who hacked him."

"Somehow, I think that if we found out who had hacked him, that would lead to the killer."

"How do you figure?"

"Because here's what I think. I think somebody hacked him so he would remove his surveillance equipment from his office and then replaced his surveillance equipment with surveillance equipment of their own. And I have a feeling I know where that surveillance equipment was."

"What are you thinking?"

"I need to make a motion to the court to have that lamp inspected." I nodded. "I think that lamp has more answers for us than we know."

CHAPTER 25
MARCH 23

"OKAY, LET'S DO THIS."

I had information I needed to make sure Damien's trial went well. There were several people I wanted to break down on the stand, because I knew the lamp used to kill Josh was also the lamp used to survey Josh's office. I discovered this when I had the lamp inspected. The only thing was, I had not yet figured out who put that surveillance equipment in there. That was what I was trying to figure out. If I could just figure that out, I would have my suspect.

I would just have to prepare as much for trial as I could. That way I could figure out the questions to ask each witness that could possibly lead the jury to know who might've done this.

Damien and I were in the conference room, preparing for trial. I had a list of witnesses who the opposing counsel, Nick Wright, would call. I had listed my witnesses as well. I knew a couple of them I would have to treat as hostile, including the governor and the governor's wife.

In particular, I was interested in the governor's wife. She

had a piece of information I knew would possibly be the key to this entire thing. Both the governor and the governor's wife had reasons to kill Josh and reasons to hate Damien. That was something else I found during the course of my investigation. I would have to bring these motives out to the jury, the best I could.

I had everything spread out in the conference room. It was like our war room. All the discovery we had gotten from the other attorney, Nick Wright, was spread out on the conference table. I had pictures of the witnesses. I had their forensic evidence. I had copies of their depositions. I also had all information Tom had given me. I hoped I was ready for trial. I prayed I was ready for trial.

Damien's life depended on me.

Damien, for his part, seemed to be not overly worried about the entire thing. As he told me, he knew he could survive prison. He had done it once before. The thing that upset him, of course, was the possibility of leaving his children. I had assured him I would take very good care of them, which put his mind to ease a bit, but, considering the stakes, he worried very much for their welfare.

"Here's who Nick will call for trial," I said. "First of all, he'll call the medical examiner. We know she'll testify Josh was killed by a blow to the head by an Oriental lamp in his office."

The killer was very bright in putting the surveillance equipment in that lamp. The lamp was a gift, I found out, from an anonymous person. Josh just apparently put the lamp in his office on the day Damien came to visit him, and, from what I found out, Josh had scheduled to have the lamp itself taken to an expert to see if it had a bug in it. He never got a chance to do that because Damien had gone to the office and somebody else used that very lamp to kill him. That was bad luck for Josh. As it turned out, it was also bad luck for Damien, because the surveillance equipment inside the lamp captured him threatening to kill Josh, and Josh screaming "what are you doing with that thing?" And I knew the thing in question was the lamp.

The fact the surveillance in the lamp had captured Damien's voice threatening Josh looked bad for us. And I knew what happened after Damien threatened to kill his father. The real killer came in, used the lamp to kill Josh, and then took the surveillance video and spliced it. They did such a good job that it was nearly impossible to tell it had been edited. I, however, knew it had been edited. It had been edited to seem as if Damien killed Josh with a lamp because it captured the audio and not the video. If they captured the video, it would've been obvious that Damien did not actually kill Josh with the lamp. However, the audio made it seem like that was exactly what happened. It had been edited to seem that way.

Therefore, one of the witnesses I would have to call was an expert to testify to this very thing. My expert's name was Jordan Smith. He told me definitively that the audio that had been captured by the surveillance inside the lamp had been altered. I would call him only if I needed to. I, of course, would try to have the surveillance audio thrown out prior to trial on a motion *in limine*.

My expert was just one of the people I was calling. I would also call Sarah, because I still had my doubts about her. I still thought maybe she was behind it all. I would call the governor's wife and the governor himself. The governor, of course, had tried to quash his subpoena with the excuse that his governmental duties precluded him from testifying at trial. However, I made a motion to compel him to testify, and Judge Grant granted the motion. The upshot was the governor himself would have to testify. He wasn't above the law and wasn't above testifying in a murder trial.

The prosecutor's witnesses would be the officers on the scene, the medical examiner, the forensic expert who matched Damien's fingerprints with that on the lamp, and that was it. Those were the only witnesses Nick would call. I doubted Nick's side of the trial would take very long.

I also knew they wanted to talk to Olivia, but, since she was on my witness list, Nick just decided to cross-examine her instead of calling her as his own witness. I guessed that was just because he was lazy, and didn't want to bother with having to subpoena her for his side.

"Okay, here's what we have to look out for with Olivia. I'm going to call her and treat her as hostile. I still think she knows more than what she's letting on and I hope that when I get her on the stand she doesn't lie. I think she was lying to me when I went to see her but she knows the penalty for perjury, doesn't she?"

Damien nodded. "I hate that my mother is so sneaky and someone we can't trust, but it is what it is. And yes, she knows the penalty for perjury. Do I think she cares? No, I don't. My mom doesn't think about things like that. She thinks she can get away with lying on the stand and she probably can. So you'll have to figure out a way to break her down so she tells the truth."

"And Sarah? Will she tell the truth on the stand?"

"No. Sarah's somebody I really can't trust. She hates me and will do anything to make sure I fry. So no, I don't think she'll be truthful on the stand."

I had struggled with whether or not I wanted to tell Damien about Sarah's being raped by Josh and Josh impregnating her. And about Sarah's having an abortion. I knew that would devastate Damien so I chose not to say anything to him about it. But trial was almost here, so I knew I would have to say something about it.

"Damien, there's something I have to tell you."

"What is it?"

I didn't quite know how to come out with this. I didn't know how he would react. He would probably be angry I kept it from him and I didn't blame him.

I took a deep breath. "Well, there's something I'm going to have to ask Sarah on the stand. There's something she did that is pretty serious, and is part of the reason why I think maybe she killed him."

"What is that?"

I took another deep breath. "As you know, she worked for Josh one summer. And, as you know, she quit abruptly. She was trying to get dirt on Josh and that was why she worked for him. I thought it odd she would just quit before she could get what she was looking for."

"And?" Damien asked. "What was that thing? Why did she quit?"

I sighed. "Damien, Josh raped her."

Damien put his head in his hands. "I knew that. At least, I suspected that. I suspected that when you told me she quit. That's the kind of person my father was. I'm not surprised but I'm upset for Sarah. I know she's my ex-wife, and we don't speak, but there's still a part of me that cares for her. And I'm very pissed she would go through something like that. I'm pissed on her behalf."

My heart was pounding. "There's more."

"What? What do you mean there's more?"

I took another deep breath, but it did little good. My nerves were completely raw. "Well, Sarah was pregnant and thought there was a possibility Josh was the father of her child. So she had an abortion."

Damien looked at me for several minutes. It was slowly dawning on him what I was telling him. He put his head in his hands and I heard him cry softly. "Do you mean to tell me there's a possibility Sarah killed my child? Is that what you're telling me?"

"Yes. I'm so sorry. I didn't know how to tell you. There was never a good time to bring this up. But I knew I had to now because I have to ask her about it on the stand. It gives her a motive for having killed him."

Damien looked stunned. "I suppose it does. I suppose it gives her motive for killing Josh." He put his hands in front of him, clasping them tightly. I could see his knuckles turning white. Then he ran his fingers through his hair and hung his head again. "It gives her motive for killing him. And it gives me a motive to kill her. She has taken so much from me. So much. And now you're telling me she took away something else? How could you keep something like that from me? How could you do that, Harper? "

"Damien, I –"

He looked defeated. "I wish I didn't know what you just told me. I wish I never had to find out something like that."

I put my arm around him but stiffened his shoulders.

"Don't, just don't. Don't try to comfort me on this." Then I looked in his eyes and saw he was enraged. It was a look I had seen before in my clients. Some of my clients had what I would term wild eyes – eyes of somebody hunted and haunted. They were the eyes of somebody beaten down his whole life, and he had had enough. They were the eyes of somebody who could kill.

The eyes of somebody who could kill right now.

Then, just as soon as the look came into his eyes, it was gone. His new expression was neutral. "Okay, let's do this."

"Damien, you can take a moment to grieve. What I just told you had to have been devastating."

"Oh, it was. What you just told me was probably one of the most devastating things I could find out at this point in time. But there's nothing I can do about it. I can't bring back the life she took. But I can try to make her pay if she killed my father. So, if that's what we need to do, that's what we'll have to do."

"Well that's what we'll do, work to make her pay if she's killed your father. I'm still not certain about that. I think maybe she was, but, I have to admit, there's somebody I think is even more likely."

That somebody was Charlene Weston.

The governor's wife.

―

CHAPTER 26

MARCH 5 - THE DAY OF THE TRIAL

IT WAS a day of the trial, and I had to admit I was extremely nervous. I had some good ideas as to who I would have to break, but had no idea if I could actually break them on the stand. I didn't know if I could show the jury that Damien was innocent of this.

The reason why I was so concerned was that I never proved to myself that Damien actually was innocent. That was always something in the back of my mind. The evidence still pointed to him. I had to admit to that. I had my suspicions about other people who had likely done this but I still wasn't sold on any of them. I hated to think my associate, Damien, would be capable of this, but I couldn't escape it. I couldn't get over the nagging thoughts I had about him. I'd seen in his eyes when I told him about Sarah's abortion that he was capable of killing somebody. And he did, when he was a young boy. He killed his stepfather. I couldn't get around that.

Nevertheless, I would have to give it my all. I would have to treat this like just another murder case. That meant I would have to break down the witnesses as best I could and bring my own evidence to show Damien didn't do this.

I hoped and prayed I could succeed.

Damien met me at the courthouse. He no longer looked defeated like he did the other day. He looked strong, purposeful. He looked like he would try to beat this down. And he had to. If he didn't, he would spend the rest of his life in prison.

I had to admit he looked extremely handsome. This was a good thing, because, after all, the jury would have a lot of women on it. He was dressed in a suit that was tailored and dark navy blue. He had on a colorful tie and his shoes were shined perfectly. He had recently gotten a haircut and it was a flattering one. He looked good in short hair. I was starting to think his hair was getting a little out of control so I was happy to see he went with a clean-cut look. He was clean-shaven and had put on a little bit of weight after having lost a good 20 pounds from the stress of preparing for trial.

"Looking spiffy," I said to him.

"Thanks. I hope it helps me."

"You know it does. You know as well as I do that members of the jury are swayed by things like how the defendant looks. And you look good."

Damien blushed a little and smiled. "I hope you're ready for this."

"You know I am." And that was the truth. I had turned over every stone and was ready to go.

Still, it was a bit nerve-racking. These cases always were. Everything was on the line – Damien's life, the fate of his family, everything. I couldn't lose this one. More than any case I have ever had, losing this one would devastate me.

. . .

We got to the courtroom and there were crowds of people milling about. Damien smiled. "Showtime," he said with a smile. "This is your wheelhouse. This is where you shine, Harper. You're one of the best at picking a jury."

I supposed he was right. In this case, it was important to get a jury composed of more than a few women. Not just because Damien was an extremely handsome man but also because the victim was a slimy sexual predator. If nothing else, I could make them hate the victim so there would be a possibility of jury nullification. In other words, there was a possibility that even if the jury decided Damien killed his father, they might still find him not guilty. Jury nullification occasionally worked, but I didn't want to count on that.

At some point, Nick Wright came in the courtroom and then Judge Grant also appeared. The potential jury panel was not yet in the courtroom, as they were waiting in another room to be called. Judge Grant wanted to speak with us before the jury was picked.

"Okay guys," Judge Grant said to us, "the case of State vs. Harrington is scheduled for today. We're scheduled to begin picking a jury today on this case. I understand from the pretrial conference that there won't be a plea agreement. So I needed to know if there are any motions *in limine* that either of the counselors want to bring or any other motions I need to hear before jury selection begins."

"Yes," Nick said. "I filed a motion *in limine* to have any evidence about the victim's sexual predation to be excluded. As you can see from my motion, I feel that any such evidence would be more prejudicial than probative. I also do not believe it's relevant to the case."

I knew that one was a nonstarter. Not only was Judge Grant a card-carrying feminist, so I knew she knew such evidence would be highly relevant in this case, but I also knew I had a good answer for it. Indeed, my entire defense might rely upon the victim's perversion. It certainly would be relevant if I tried to show Sarah killed Josh. For now, that was my best bet. Although I also had another long-shot suspect, and that was the governor's wife. In the case of the governor's wife, the fact that Josh was a slimy bastard was highly relevant.

Judge Grant looked over at me, and appeared to roll her eyes. "What say you counselor? What's your reason for bringing evidence of the victim's predation?"

And then she looked at my response to Nick's motion *in limine* and she nodded her head. "Never mind, I see it's relevant because you plan on bringing in alternative suspects who were on the wrong end of the victim's sexual perversion. I'm going to deny the motion *in limine*, and allow limited inquiry into Mr. Roland's proclivity toward sexual harassment and sexual assault. By limited, I mean you, Ms. Ross, may only inquire about Mr. Roland's sexual predation as it applies to your witnesses. You are not to bring in other instances where he perhaps harassed or assaulted women."

I knew she would rule in such a way. There was no way she could keep something like this out.

"I, too, have a motion *in limine*," I said to the judge. "In this case, I'm looking to include evidence, not exclude it. I specifically want to make sure that one of my witnesses can testify her father's suicide was a result of bad actions the victim took against her father. As you can see in my motion, when one of my suspects, Sarah White, was only 10 years old, her father killed himself because his business went bankrupt directly because Mr. Roland refused to honor a contract Mr. White made with him to build some apartment buildings. In this case, it was a personal contract between Mr. Roland and Mr. White, not a contract between Mr. Roland's business and Mr. White. I plan on showing a but-for causation between Mr. Roland's action and Mr. White's suicide. That gives Ms. White another reason to want to kill Mr. Roland."

Judge Grant appeared to look over my motion to have the evidence included and then looked over at Nick. "Mr. Wright, I'm inclined to grant her motion, do you have any objections to this motion?"

"Again, this evidence is more prejudicial than probative, however, I have no objection."

"Okay, I'll allow it. Do you two have anything else for me?"

"I have two more motions," I said. "One is to have my client's juvenile record excluded, and one is to have the audio recording that has my client threatening the victim should also be excluded."

"Well," Judge Grant said. "It goes without saying your client's juvenile record isn't relevant. I see it's been unsealed. How the hell did that happen?" She shook her head. "Whatever. That's not relevant, so I'll exclude it."

Nick opened his mouth and then shut it again. It was as if he wanted to protest.

Judge Grant looked at Nick with a weary expression. "You wanted to say something, counselor?"

"I answered Ms. Ross' motion *in limine* on this," he said. "In my defense, I stated that Mr. Harrington's juvenile record is admissible because it goes to motive. We won't be bringing it in to show the Defendant was acting in accordance with his juvenile behavior."

"Motive, huh?" Judge Grant reviewed Nick's response to my motion.

"Yes, motive. His juvenile record shows Mr. Harrington killed to protect his mother. That was why he killed his stepfather. Once again, we believe Mr. Harrington killed Josh Roland to protect the people he loved - his best friend from prosecution and his daughter from molestation. That's his motive for killing

Mr. Roland, that and the fact that Mr. Roland raped his mother."

"I see." Judge Grant said. "A very creative argument, Mr. Wright. I'm impressed. But I'm still not going to allow it." Then she looked down. "As to the audio that allegedly caught Mr. Harrington threatening Mr. Roland, it looks like Ms. Ross has done her homework on that tape. She's hired an expert who can testify the audio has been altered. For that reason alone, I won't allow that audio to be played. It apparently hasn't been authenticated."

Nick looked at me, a pissed-off look on his face. "Your honor, the audio has been authenticated."

"Well, I'm seeing a sworn affidavit here from a Jordan Smith, a forensic expert specializing in audio recordings, and he has indicated the audio has been doctored. I won't taint the jury with a tainted audio, so my ruling stands."

"But your honor," Nick protested, "defense counsel is free to call the audio into question with her expert on the stand."

"Counselor," Judge Grant said, "you know very good and well that the jury will be influenced by that audio even if an expert took the stand to testify it was doctored. Sorry, but I won't let that horse out of the barn. Now, Mr. Wright, do you have any other motion for me to entertain?"

"No, your honor." Nick was pouting and I was inwardly celebrating.

Suck it, Wright.

"Ms. Ross?"

"Nothing, your honor."

"Okay, then, we'll get this show on the road. I'll start bringing in the jury panel."

· · ·

Jury selection was next, and I think I did a good job with it. I managed to get a jury with seven women and five men, including at least one woman that indicated she had been a victim of sexual harassment. In today's climate, I didn't think it would be so unusual to find a woman who got on the wrong end of a man like Josh.

With a jury selected, it was time to begin.

CHAPTER 27

Nick was the first to go. He opted to do his opening statement in one chunk as opposed to taking part of the time to do his opening statement before I spoke and part of the time afterward.

I'd seen Nick in action before because I had cases with him several times. He was deliberate, calm and cool and could look every jury member in the eye and make each of them feel as if he was speaking directly to them. He had a gift for persuasion and I knew I would have to up my game in my opening statement. I also thought he liked to show off. He liked the game. And that's what it was for him, a game. Even though he knew Damien well and liked him, that didn't matter. He just wanted to win.

Nick went up to the jury box, and addressed each juror. "Ladies and gentlemen of the jury, thank you very much for your time. That's the first thing I wanted to say, because I know that each of you would want to be doing something different with your time today. Not many of you would choose to serve on a jury if you had the choice. I wanted you to know how much I appreciate your time and attention."

He sighed and hung his head. "This is a hard one for me, I'm not gonna lie. Damien Harrington, who stands accused of murder, is a colleague and friend. When I first found out he had been accused of murdering his father, I didn't want to believe it. But, as I got more into the case, I realized the facts were staring at me in the face. And the conclusion was inescapable – Damien killed his father in cold blood."

"Now, did Mr. Harrington possibly have a reason to kill his father? The defense will tell you he did. They're going to tell you Josh was a terrible person - he was a sexual predator and cheated people in business. That may or may not be true. But even if it were true, under the law it would not matter. All you need to be focused on is the fact that Mr. Harrington went to his father's office on November 6 of last year and confronted him about an incident he was angry about. He had found out his best friend, Nick Savante, was possibly going back to prison for allegedly stealing from Mr. Roland. Mr. Savante was never formally charged, so Mr. Harrington reasonably deduced the charges were trumped up and that made him very angry. He had also found out that Mr. Roland had molested his daughter. Mr. Roland raped his own mother, which was how Mr. Harrington was conceived. Mr. Harrington is the kind who will do anything to protect the people he loves, and that means anything – even murder. Mr. Harrington went to Mr. Roland's office on November 6. At that time, Mr. Harrington was angry enough to kill him. In fact it's what he did. Mr. Harrington killed Mr. Roland with Mr. Roland's own lamp. It was a heavy lamp, made of solid brass. Mr. Harrington picked up that lamp, swung at Mr. Roland, and hit him in the head. He swung at him with such force that he killed him instantly."

Nick went on.

"And we know Mr. Harrington killed Mr. Roland for one reason. There was one set of fingerprints on that lamp. Well, actually that's a lie – there were two sets of fingerprints on that lamp, and one of those sets of fingerprints belonged to Mr. Roland. The other set belonged to Mr. Harrington. There were no other fingerprints that can be matched on that lamp. You'll hear evidence about this."

"So there you have it ladies and gentlemen. An open and shut case really. Mr. Harrington had motive to kill Mr. Roland – Mr. Roland raped his mother and molested his daughter. Mr. Roland was threatening to send his best friend back to prison. Let's face it, the molestation alone would give almost anybody motive to kill Mr. Roland. And I am sympathetic to Mr. Harrington. I really am. A part of me doesn't blame him for doing what he did. But the law is clear, ladies and gentlemen. The law is clear that if you kill somebody in cold blood, then you must be guilty of murder in the first degree. And let me remind you that deliberation in the case of murder in the first degree can be a split second. A split-second when you had the presence of mind to kill somebody."

The split-second thing was important because it gave me one avenue to try for an acquittal. If anything, I could prove to the jury that Damien couldn't have killed in cold blood, because, according to the facts presented by the prosecutor, it would be a heat of passion murder, if nothing else. That would mean a lesser charge – perhaps second-degree murder or manslaughter. Since the prosecutor in this case chose not to charge Damien with lesser offenses, only first degree murder, I could get Damien acquitted by showing he didn't deliberate on whether to kill Josh, even for a moment.

That was a fallback position, but, of course, my job was to make the jury see Damien didn't do it. And that was how I would have to approach my opening statement.

I approached the jury. And I looked all of them in the eye. I took a deep breath. And then just took a moment to look at them. I wanted them to look at my eyes and hopefully see the honesty in my soul. That was always my way of approaching jurors.

I cocked my head. "Ladies and gentlemen, the prosecutor, Mr. Wright, hinted as to what kind of person the victim, Josh Roland, was." I nodded. "He hinted, but let me tell you what kind of person he was. He was a sexual predator. He raped numerous women, he molested at least one child, and he harassed numerous women. In other words, there were many people who had motive to kill him. My client, Damien Harrington, had the least motive to kill him of all the people you will see on the stand today. You will hear testimony from Olivia Ward, who is Mr. Harrington's mother. She will testify that Mr. Roland raped her when she was only 15 years old. And she hated him for that reason. You will hear testimony from Sarah White, the ex-wife of Mr. Harrington. She will testify that Mr. Roland raped and impregnated her and she had an abortion because of this. She will also testify that when she was 10 years old her father killed himself because of Mr. Roland. You see, Mr. Roland, in addition to being a sexual predator, was also a business cheat. He made a contract with Ms. White's father, Martin White, to build some apartment buildings. He refused to pay Mr. White the money he owed him, which led Mr. White to filing for bankruptcy for his company. That, in turn, led Mr. White to suicide. So, as you can see, Sarah White had double reasons to kill Josh Roland."

"Sarah and Olivia are not the only people with reasons to kill Josh Roland. You will hear evidence the governor of the state, Governor Weston, also had reason to kill Mr. Roland. Mr. Roland had information about the governor that could have led to the governor serving years in prison. So the governor had reason to kill Mr. Roland to protect his secret. And, finally, another individual who had reason to kill Josh Roland is the wife of the governor. Addison Weston is the wife of Governor Weston and the First Lady of the State of Missouri. She was also having an affair with Josh Roland. You'll hear evidence that Addison Weston wanted to leave her husband to be with Mr. Roland. You'll hear evidence that Mr. Roland had no interest in doing the same. That, in fact, Addison Weston somehow thought she was the only woman in his life, but that was far from the truth."

"You will also hear evidence that Addison Weston was angry with Mr. Harrington. And that would be why she made it seem as if Damien killed Mr. Roland, when she might've been the person who actually killed him. The reason why she was angry with Damien is because she wanted to divorce her husband. She wanted to divorce her husband, and wanted to make sure her husband was humiliated. She wanted a very good settlement from her husband. Mr. Harrington took that away from her."

"You will hear evidence that Mr. Harrington took away her ability to divorce her husband and get an excellent settlement while humiliating him in the process. And that is really the bottom line. Because the person who killed Mr. Roland not only had a motive to kill Mr. Roland, but also must've been angry with my client, Mr. Harrington. Because, after all, Mr. Harrington was framed by the person who killed Mr. Roland. You will find everybody who I will call had a serious problem with Mr. Roland and a serious problem with my client. Sarah White is Mr. Harrington's ex-wife. Mr. Harrington unceremoniously asked her to leave the house, and that made Sarah White extremely angry with my client. Olivia Ward, my client's mother, also has reason to frame her own son. You will hear evidence that my client, Damien, has not exactly been a model son. In fact, he ignored her for many years. The governor not only has reason to be angry with Josh Roland, but also with my client. You'll hear evidence that my client obtained a commutation of a sentence for his friend, in exchange for covering up the fact the governor has homosexual tendencies. That evidence is also the reason why Addison Weston has reason to be angry with my client."

I knew there would be a risk in admitting in court that Damien had blackmailed the governor. I knew that. However, I also knew it would be important - it would be important to show why the governor and his wife both had reason to be angry with Damien. It gave them motive to frame him. In the end, I decided it was more important to show motive to the governor and his wife and had to balance that against the risk Damien might be in trouble for blackmail.

"So you see, plenty of people had reasons to want Josh dead. And by the time these individuals testify, you will understand there is reasonable doubt that my client killed Josh Roland. And that's all you need to acquit. Reasonable doubt. That means that in your mind it is more likely than not that my client did not kill his father."

"Now, there is the issue of the lamp. I admit my client's fingerprints were on that lamp. However, I'll submit to you that the actual killer used that lamp to kill Josh Roland and frame my client for doing so. The real killer came in after my client went into Josh Roland's office to confront him, and the real killer used gloves to pick up that lamp and bludgeon Josh Roland to death."

"You'll hear evidence there was surveillance equipment found inside the lamp, surveillance equipment that was so small that it was not detected until I made a motion to inspect the lamp and had an expert inspect it as well. You'll hear evidence from the expert, Jordan Smith, that there was surveillance equipment inside that lamp."

The only thing about the fact there was surveillance equipment inside the lamp was I couldn't ascertain who put the surveillance equipment there. I knew it was in there but it could've been put in there by anybody. That was why I'd have to get somebody on the record and ask them about it. Maybe somebody would admit to it.

"So you see, ladies and gentlemen, there were many different people who wanted Josh Roland dead. And here's what happened. Somebody put surveillance equipment inside that lamp, and that somebody knew Damien had picked up that lamp and brandished it against Josh Roland. But the key word here is brandished against him – what that means is that, yes, Damien was angry with Josh Roland, and, yes, Damien picked up the lamp and swung it at Josh Roland. He did that. However, Damien checked his swing and did not actually make physical contact with Josh Roland. He put the lamp down after he swung it at him and then left the office. When he left the office, Mr. Roland was alive. And that's what happened."

"You will see evidence about everything I just told you. And you will conclude there is enough doubt that my client killed his father that you will have to acquit. I ask for a verdict of not guilty. Thank you very much."

I sat down and the judge addressed the jury. "Okay, ladies and gentlemen of the jury, we've had the opening statements. It's now time for a break. Come back in 20 minutes."

The jury filed out and I looked at Damien. "Well, what do you think?"

Damien let out a sigh. "I hope you know what you're doing. I really do."

I knew Damien had problems with my strategy. I didn't blame him, either. After all, I would be admitting to the court that Damien had blackmailed the governor. That was a risk. I also would admit Damien had brandished the lamp against Josh. That didn't look good. Yet I had to admit to those things to get to the heart of my case. There was no way around any of it. If I didn't show these things, I couldn't show why the real killer knew to frame Damien.

"Damien, don't worry. I know what I'm doing."

Damien looked at me with haunted eyes. Then he shook his head. "My life is in your hands. You know that."

"I know that. I understand that. And am I sure we'll win the case?" I shook my head. "No, I don't want to lie to you and say I'm sure of it. This will be one of the more difficult cases I've had. But, I'm completely prepared for this case. And I'm going to give it my all. You can count on that. And, trust me on this, I have won more cases than I've lost."

Damien still looked extremely worried. "I know. I understand you have to do what you have to do. I understand your logic. I just hope it doesn't boomerang on us."

"I know, I know. I hope and pray the same thing."

CHAPTER 28

In 20 minutes, the jury came back. They all took a seat and prepared to listen to us for the rest of the afternoon. They all looked interested in this case. That was a good thing, because I often saw juries who looked completely bored. Not that I blamed them. I knew that if I was a juror, I would be bored. To say the least.

"Okay, counselor, call your first witness," Judge Grant said.

"The State calls Officer Richard O'Neill."

Officer O'Neill was the officer on the scene. He examined the crime scene, spoke with the witnesses, and ended up making Damien's arrest.

Officer O'Neill was a tall man with red hair and a ruddy complexion. He always had a smile on his face and that endeared him to most people.

He approached the bench, and was sworn in. He stated his name, and Nick went to work.

"Okay Officer O'Neill," Nick said. "Can you please tell the jury what your position is with the Kansas City Police Department?"

"I am an Officer with the Kansas City Police Department."

"And what is your role in this case?"

"I was the first one at the scene. I was the first one at Mr. Roland's office after I was called by Mr. Roland's Secretary, Jacqueline Peterson. She dialed 911 and I was the officer in the area, so I was the first responder."

"Ms. Peterson called you? Is that what you're saying?"

"Yes, that was why I was called to Mr. Roland's office."

"What was your understanding as to why Ms. Peterson contacted 911?"

I knew Jacqueline Peterson would be testifying for the prosecution later on so I didn't object to any kind of hearsay she might've said to the officer. I'd have a chance to cross-examine her later.

"It was my understanding that Ms. Peterson had concerns about a fight she heard between Mr. Harrington and Mr. Roland."

"I see. And what did she say?"

"Ms. Peterson had heard words between Mr. Harrington and Mr. Roland. She said at first she did not go into the office to see what happened. She was busy with work that day. But about an hour later, she went into the office and found Mr. Roland dead on the floor. It was at that point that she called 911 and I was the officer on the scene."

"What time were you called to the scene?"

"I was called to the scene at 2:15 in the afternoon."

"When you got to the scene what did you find?"

"I found the deceased, Mr. Josh Roland, lying on the floor. The back of his head had been bludgeoned with a heavy object. Next to the body was a heavy lamp."

"Could you please describe the lamp?"

"It was an Oriental lamp. It was white and was decorated with pictures of Chinese men and women and flowers."

"I would like to show you what is been marked as Exhibit A. Could you please look at this picture and tell me if this is the lamp you found on the floor next to the body of Josh Roland?"

At that, Nick handed officer O'Neill a picture of the lamp used to kill Josh.

"Yes, that is a picture of the lamp I saw lying next to Mr. Roland's body."

"Besides the body of Mr. Roland, did you see anybody else around the scene?"

"No, I did not."

"After you arrived at the scene, and you saw the body on the floor, what did you do?"

"I processed the lamp for fingerprints."

"When you say you processed the lamp for fingerprints, can you please explain to the court what you mean by that?"

"When I process a crime scene for fingerprints, I use a fiber-glass brush to dust a bi-chromatic powder on surface areas. This powder has both black and white pigmentations."

"Did you process the lamp you found at the crime scene in this manner?"

"Yes, I did."

"Did you take a picture of the fingerprint you found on the lamp?"

"Yes, I did."

"Were you able to match this fingerprint with an individual in your database?"

"Yes, I was able to match that fingerprint with Mr. Harrington."

"I have nothing further for this witness."

Judge Grant looked at me. "Counselor, do you have any questions for this witness?"

"Yes, Your Honor." I approached the witness. "Officer

O'Neill," I began. "You stated you were called to the scene at approximately 2:15 in the afternoon, is that correct?"

"Yes, that's correct."

"And you stated the reason why you are called to the scene was because Jacqueline Peterson had called 911, because she was concerned that two individuals were fighting in Mr. Roland's office and later went into Mr. Roland's office and found him dead. Is that correct?"

"Yes, that's correct."

"Did Ms. Peterson happen to tell you what time Mr. Harrington was in Mr. Roland's office?"

"No, she didn't volunteer information about that."

"Did you question her about when Mr. Harrington was in his office?" I was trying to pin down the officer, because I had a feeling he did not get information he needed to get from Jacqueline Peterson about when Damien was in the office. According to Damien, he had left the office at 1:15 that afternoon.

"Yes, I did get that information."

"And what did she tell you about when Mr. Harrington was in his office?"

"She told me Mr. Harrington had an appointment to see Mr. Roland at 1 o'clock in the afternoon."

"And did she tell you what time Mr. Harrington left the office?"

"Yes she did. She stated she saw Mr. Harrington leave Mr. Roland's office in a huff around 2 o'clock in the afternoon."

That was a problem, of course. A problem I would have to address with Jacqueline when she came on the stand. I would have to heavily cross-examine her on when Damien left the building, because she apparently told the officer something incorrect about when he left. I knew this, because I read it in the police report, but I wanted to see if the officer would say something different on the stand.

The timing was so important, because the time of death had been calculated to be around 2 PM that day. So Jacqueline was really an indispensable witness for me. But only if I could get her to admit on the stand she had seen Damien leave earlier than what she originally thought.

"And you told the court you dusted for fingerprints and the fingerprints on the murder weapon matched my client, correct?"

"Yes, that's correct."

I opened my mouth to ask him why he was able to match up the fingerprints so quickly, but then I realized something. The reason why they could match the fingerprint so quickly was because Damien's fingerprints were in the system. Which meant, of course, he had been arrested at least once. Since I didn't want the jury to know this fact, I decided to leave well enough alone.

I decided there was limited value in cross-examining this officer further, so I decided to rest. "I have nothing further for this witness, Your Honor."

"Counselor," the Judge Grant said to Nick. "Do you have anything further for this witness?"

"No, Your Honor."

"The witness is excused. Mr. Wright, please call your next witness."

"The State calls Jacqueline Peterson to the stand."

Jacqueline Peterson approached the witness stand. She was about 25, blonde curly hair, a fair complexion and brown eyes. She was dressed in a floor-length skirt and a shirt buttoned up to her neck. She was a large woman, about 6 feet tall, and built like a brick shithouse. She looked like she worked out with heavy weights. It was odd seeing somebody so large trying to look so dainty, with her demure skirt and shirt.

She sat down, was sworn in, stated her name for the record, and Nick got down to business.

"Ms. Peterson, could you please tell the court your position with Aragon International?"

"I was an executive assistant to Mr. Josh Roland."

"And as an executive assistant, what are your basic duties?"

"I type up dictated correspondence and answer phones for Mr. Roland."

"And where is your office located, in relation to Mr. Roland's office?"

"My office is adjacent to Mr. Roland's office."

"By adjacent, what do you mean?"

"It means my office is connected to his office."

"Does that mean you can hear what is going on in Mr. Roland's office?"

"Yes, I can sometimes."

I knew I could trip her up on her testimony. I knew there was one thing executives do not like, and that would be having an office that wasn't soundproof. I'd actually tested the office and found it was soundproof. So I knew she was lying. There was no way she could hear Damien and Josh arguing.

"And on the day you found your boss murdered, did you hear an argument coming from Mr. Roland's office?"

"Yes I did."

"Did you understand what the argument was about?"

"No, I just know there where words spoken between the two men that were harsh. To say the very least."

"Now, tell the court about how you found the body of Mr. Roland?"

"Well, here's what happened. I was very busy that day and heard the two men arguing, but I didn't try to disturb them. I saw Mr. Harrington leave Mr. Roland's office and he seemed very angry. When he came into the office, he seemed angry as well. I've seen Mr. Harrington before and he's always been very kind to me. Very friendly. But on this day, when he came into the office, he had a very mean look on his face. I greeted him and he did not say anything back to me. Which was unusual. And when he left the office, he left in a fury. His fists were clenched and he looked like he was itching for a fight."

"Objection, Your Honor, this witness is not responding to the question."

"Sustained. Ms. Peterson, please answer the question posed to you, and not another question."

Jacqueline looked flustered. "I was getting to it. I was getting around to how I found the body."

Judge Grant rolled her eyes. "Be that as it may, Ms. Peterson, the prosecuting attorney is asking you a specific question. The question he asked you is how you discovered the body. He did not ask you about Mr. Harrington's demeanor or how Mr. Harrington usually treats you, or any of that. Please answer the specific question and wait for another one." Judge Grant looked annoyed she had to instruct the witness on such elementary matters. I guessed Nick had no time to prepare this witness for her testimony - either that or she just liked the spotlight. At any rate, Judge Grant was losing patience with her. That much I could tell.

Jacqueline looked at the judge. "Do you want me to answer the question?"

"Yes, please answer the question."

Jacqueline still looked nervous. "Well, as I said, I was busy that day, and I heard the two men arguing. I was meaning to check on them, and I did, a little after 2 o'clock in the afternoon. I walked in and saw Josh lying on the floor. I saw the lamp was next to him, he wasn't moving, and there was a lot of blood. I checked to see if there was a pulse. There was none. I screamed but then called 911 immediately."

"When did you see Mr. Harrington leave the office?"

"I saw him leave the office right before I went into the office and discovered Mr. Roland on the floor."

"And would you please describe to the court his demeanor as he left the office?"

"As I said before, he was very tense and mean. He had closed fists and I tried to say goodbye to him, but he just walked on, without even acknowledging me. I didn't know what I did wrong, but that was how he acted."

"Do you still work for Aragon International?"

"No, I don't. I quit right after I found Mr. Roland dead. I couldn't go back after that." She hung her head.

"I have nothing further for this witness."

"Ms. Ross, do you have anything for this witness?" Judge Grant asked me.

"I do, Your Honor." I approached the witness on the stand. "Ms. Peterson, you stated on direct that Mr. Harrington, my client, arrived at the office to speak with Mr. Roland, and it seemed like he was itching for a fight. Is that correct?"

"Yes, that's correct."

"And what time did Mr. Harrington arrive at the office to speak with Mr. Roland?"

Jacqueline looked at the ceiling. "I think it was about 1 o'clock in the afternoon."

I nodded. "1 o'clock in the afternoon. Did Mr. Harrington have an appointment to see Mr. Roland?"

"No. He did not. He just showed up at the office looking very angry."

"He looked very angry? And yet you didn't try to stop him from seeing Mr. Roland?"

She shook her head. "No, I didn't try to stop him from seeing Mr. Roland."

"Ms. Peterson, is it your job to prevent people from seeing Mr. Roland during the day? I mean, are you the person who makes appointments for Mr. Roland and ushers people into the office when they show up for an appointment?"

"Yes, that was my job."

"Yet, my client shows up, looking very angry, and you didn't do anything to stop him from going into the office. Is that what you're trying to say?"

She looked unsure of herself. "I guess. I mean, I was really busy that day and wanted to stop him from seeing Mr. Roland, but there were so many things going on at that time that I just didn't."

"Is that something you've gotten into a habit with? Just letting people go in to see Mr. Roland willy-nilly?"

"Well, it's unfair to say it's willy-nilly. I do try to vet people who show up to see Mr. Roland."

I nodded. "Okay, now your testimony on direct was that your office was adjacent to Mr. Roland's office. And you also testified on direct that you could hear the two men quarreling. Is that correct?"

"Yes, that's right."

"Now isn't it true you really can't hear what's going on in Mr. Roland's office?"

"No that's not true."

"It's not true? Are you telling the court that Mr. Roland has an office with walls so thin you can hear him conducting his business? Is that what you're trying to say to the court?"

Now she really looked unsure. "Yes, that's true." She shifted uncomfortably in her chair. She nodded. "That's right. Mr. Roland's office is not sound-proof. I can hear what's going on in there sometimes. But only if there's a lot of screaming and shouting."

"Mr. Roland is a billionaire, or was a billionaire, and was the CEO of a multinational company. Isn't that right?"

"Yes of course that's right."

"And yet your testimony is that a man as important as Mr. Roland does not desire his privacy? That he would not sound-proof his office? That's what you're trying to tell the court?"

She nodded her head silently, but did not look like she knew the answer to this question anymore.

"Please answer verbally, and I would like to remind you the penalty for perjury."

She swallowed hard and shifted in her chair again uncomfortably. "Well, I saw Mr. Harrington was angry, so I guess I imagined they were having words. I guess I didn't actually hear them."

"That's right, you didn't hear them. Now you testified my client left Mr. Roland's office shortly before you found Mr. Roland dead, is that right?"

"Right."

"Yet you also testified on direct that you heard the two men arguing and you did not pay attention to them for a long time. You were too busy. So, isn't it true you did not actually see Mr. Harrington leave?"

"I did see him leave. I saw him leave around 2 o'clock."

"I would like to remind you about your earlier testimony. You stated you were too busy to interfere with the two men arguing. And you went to Mr. Roland's office sometime after you stopped hearing the argument. This would imply there was some time in between what you imagined were the arguments between the two men and Mr. Harrington leaving. Isn't that right?"

"I don't understand."

"If you saw my client leaving right before you went into the office to check on Mr. Roland, that would contradict what you're saying earlier. In that case, if you saw him leaving in a huff, that would imply you went into the office directly after the confrontation between the two men. Is that right?"

She looked confused. "I guess so."

"Isn't it true you don't know what time Mr. Harrington left Mr. Roland's office?" Her testimony was very confused and I was trying to bring that out to the jury.

She shook her head but didn't say anything.

"Please answer verbally."

"I think it was 2 o'clock. But now that you mention it, I was very busy that day. And you're right, I didn't go into the office until after I thought the confrontation was over. In fact, it was sometime after I thought the confrontation was over. About half-hour after that."

"A half-hour after you thought the confrontation was over was when you went into the office. Is that your current testimony?"

"Yes," she said unsurely. "That is my current testimony."

"So, in all actuality, it's more logical to assume that Mr. Harrington actually left some time before you went into Mr. Roland's office, isn't that right?"

She nodded her head. "I guess so. I mean, I guess now that I think about it, Mr. Harrington did leave sometime before I went into the office." She nodded. "I don't know, everything happened so fast. And I was so very busy that day."

"I understand. You said several times how busy you were. Now, did you actually see my client leaving Mr. Roland's office, or is it another incident you are misremembering?"

She looked up at the ceiling. "I definitely saw him come in the office, and he was very angry at that time. I know that for fact."

"But you didn't see him leave, then. Is that what you're saying?"

She shook her head. "I was so very busy that day." She looked embarrassed.

"I have nothing further for this witness."

I knew I did my job with Jacqueline. It was pretty obvious she was not as confident as she let on. She didn't actually see Damien leaving. That was extremely important. Because if she stayed on her testimony that Damien left the office about 2 PM, it would've been very bad for us on the timeline. That was because the time of death was between 1:45 PM and 2 PM.

"Mr. Wright, do you have any redirect for this witness?"

"No, Your Honor."

"Ms. Peterson, you can step down."

She hung her head and looked embarrassed as she left the courtroom.

The next few witnesses were important, but not overly so. One of the witnesses was the medical examiner. I didn't have any questions for the medical examiner except to pin her down on the time of death. She reiterated the time of death was between 1:45 and 2 PM, and that was very important to establish. It was important to establish because I knew Damien would testify that he'd left the office at around 1:15. And, considering Jacqueline Peterson admitted she didn't really know when Damien left the office, I knew we were doing well as far as the timeline went.

Of course, Nick Wright had to blow up the pictures of Josh, as he lay in a pool of blood. He blew them up for maximum effect.

After the medical examiner finished her testimony, the prosecution rested. I knew Nick was interested in Olivia's testimony, but I was calling her as my witness. Olivia was the only other person that had relevant testimony as far as the prosecution went, because nobody else really knew the dynamic between Damien and his father.

By this time, it was 5 PM. It was time for everybody to go home.

As I drove home, I looked back on that day and knew we were ahead of the game. I'd tripped up Jacqueline Peterson and made her admit she didn't really hear them arguing and didn't really know what time my client left the office. Those were two important pieces of testimony I elicited from her so I felt pretty good about our chances at that point. The other witnesses seem to be a bit of a wash and didn't really hurt or help us. So, if I was keeping a scorecard, I would say I won on one of the witnesses and pushed on the others. All in all, I felt good.

I rode home with Damien. He wanted to talk to me about how the first day went.

"I think it went well, as well as a possibly could."

"I think so too." He looked hopeful. "Tomorrow, I guess we'll have our witnesses on the stand."

"Yes, and tomorrow is when we either start to win or lose this case."

And that was the truth. This entire case rested upon whether or not I could break down one of the witnesses I had. Either Olivia, Sarah, the governor, or the First Lady, had to be broken down on the stand. That was the only way we could possibly win.

I still liked our chances though.

CHAPTER 29

That night, I went home to my girls and Axel. They were my grounding. They were what made my job worthwhile. Knowing I could come home to them was something I cherished. And, after what Abby had gone through, I cherished being with her and Rina and Axel all the more.

It was still an uphill battle with Abby. She was in the rehab center for several weeks. She missed her finals but made them up. More than that, I realized she really needed me. She needed me to be a stabilizing influence. We went through enough family counseling for me to understand that what I needed to do with Abby was to make sure she was well. I learned she became addicted to heroin pretty easily. And, according to her doctor, that was not necessarily unusual, as that particular drug was extremely addictive anyway. But the therapist told me I would have to be vigilant with her for the rest of her life. I'd always have to look for the signs she was turning to drugs.

For Rina's part, she was finally becoming nicer to her sister. The two of them had always had a bit of a love-hate relationship. A bit of a tug-of-war. It was mainly because Rina was so dominant and Abby was so submissive. The dynamics were always so skewed.

But after Abby had her problems, Rina decided to be nicer to her. What that meant was that Rina included Abby in her social activities more. Abby started making more friends and started to adjust to her school a lot better than she had before. She was not popular, exactly, but neither was she an outcast anymore. At least, that was how she explained it to me. She told me she no longer felt she was on the outside looking in but was finally on the inside.

"You know that story about the Little Match Girl?" Abby asked me one night. "Where she was standing outside in the cold looking in on the people inside the homes? And how she would imagine how life was like for them, with every match she lit? That was how I always felt in school, Mom. I always felt like I was the little match girl, my nose pressed on the glass, looking in on everybody else and wanting what they had."

"And how do you feel now, Buttercup?"

She shrugged. "I guess it's okay. I guess I don't feel like I'm such a freak anymore. Rina has encouraged her friends to be nice to me, and they've even tried to get to know me. Some of them even like me now. So, there's that."

I had to smile. "I'll always be there for you. I hope you know that. And Abby, if you need me to work less, you just need to tell me."

She just shook her head. "Thanks, Mom, but I know you have your hands full right now. I mean, Damien can't do a lot of work for you right now and I know you relied on him before. I know that with Damien gone from the office so much, your work is even more piled up than usual. I know that Mom. And I'm okay, really I am."

So that night, after the first day of trial, I really tried to do what I always did when I came home. And that was to make sure our lives were as normal as possible. That was another thing I learned from the counselor – I needed to make life more or less normal. I couldn't treat Abby like a glass doll. Like she was fragile and I was afraid of breaking her. She was resilient. I had to realize that. She was a kid. She could bounce back. And as long as I made sure I paid attention to her and learned to look for the signs of drug abuse, I knew she would be okay.

We had dinner around the table. "So, Mom, how did things go?" Abby asked me.

"Good, I think." I knew the two girls were very worried about Damien. They knew that if Damien went to prison, we would have Nate and Amelia living here. They were okay with that, actually. They were more worried about Damien and what would happen to him. The girls really loved him. He was very good with them and he loved them back.

"What do you mean, you think?" Rina demanded. "I need to hear you're kicking butt in that courtroom, Mom. And taking names. That's what I need to hear."

I smiled. I was never that confident. In any of my cases. That was one thing with me - I didn't always have confidence in myself or my abilities. No matter how many cases I won, I always felt like I was the underdog and my back was against the wall.

I certainly felt like that with Damien's case.

I tousled her hair. "Okay, okay, I'm kicking butt and taking names. I'm making the prosecutor sign his own death warrant and cry." I nodded. "Is that what you wanted to hear?"

"Yeah, Mom, that's the spirit!" Abby said. "You just have to keep up that confidence, like you're always telling me. You're always telling me to have confidence in myself. And you need to do the same thing. You need to look on the bright side. That's what you're always telling me. Look on the bright side."

I had to smile. "I'm trying but I've never felt so much pressure. This is Damien. This isn't just any other client. It's Damien. If I mess this up, he'll go down for the rest of his life. I just don't think I could live with myself."

Axel came over and rubbed my shoulders. "You got this, lass," he said.

I hoped he was right. If he wasn't, I would be haunted for the rest of my life.

Damien going to prison would haunt me like I had never been haunted before.

CHAPTER 30

The next day, I started with Olivia as my first witness. I figured I should get her out of the way. Of all the people who I figured might be an alternative suspect in this case, Olivia was my weakest one. I didn't think she was responsible for killing Josh, although I had to try to make it look like she did. My goal was just to muddy the waters. I wasn't sure about any of my witnesses but if I could just make it seem like they all could've possibly been responsible, I knew I did my job.

Olivia wasn't happy to be put on the stand. She told me that several times before I called her. She didn't come willingly, either. She had to be subpoenaed. That was fine. As long as she showed up, it was all would be okay.

She met me early at the courthouse. "I don't know why I have to put up with this bullshit," she said. "And I don't know why I'm being called."

I never did really tell Olivia why she was being called. I never wanted to admit to her that I wanted the jury to think she possibly killed Josh. If I told her that, she would've been pissed, to say the very least. She probably would've tried to fight the subpoena. After all, if I did my job well, there was a possibility the authorities might to be looking at her. That was the last thing she wanted.

I knew she would be looked at by the authorities, maybe, if I did my job right – but that wasn't my problem. I had to do what I had to do. If I had to drag everybody under the bus while doing it, I would. It wasn't like Olivia and Sarah were so pristine. And I knew that if they really didn't do it and the authorities started sniffing around, they would find, in the end, they were innocent. At least, I hoped that was the case. I sometimes had nightmares that the alternative suspects I would bring into cases would end up in trouble even though they were innocent of any wrongdoing. I lived in fear of ruining people's lives.

Still, my obligation was to my client. First, last, period.

"I told you, you're being called as a character witness." That was a lie, of course. I just had to make her comfortable. I would blindside her, I knew that. But it was better I do so. That way, I could keep her off balance, and if I kept her off balance, she might actually tell the truth. At least, that was my hope.

Olivia looked nice, for her. She was dressed in a green dress that went well with her skin tone. Her hair was tied up in a bun, as opposed to being wild, which is what it usually was. I knew when she arrived at the court that she had been drinking. But that was the usual state of affairs. She usually was drinking. It was very difficult to find a time when she wasn't drinking. I had to take what I could get.

"You have to wait outside the courtroom. I'm so sorry. But there's a thing called the rule on witnesses and that means that witnesses cannot be in the courtroom until they are called."

Olivia rolled her eyes. "Boy, this is getting better and better. Now you tell me I need to wait outside the courtroom like I'm a dog waiting to get into the house. If you hear some scratching at the door, it's just me, trying to get in. Pay it no mind."

"I'll try to remember that."

I went into the courtroom, leaving Olivia outside. She did have to wait outside, because of the rule on witnesses, but, truth be told, I really wanted her to be outside because I didn't want to deal with her at the moment. She would start asking me a lot of questions, questions I didn't really want to answer. And I knew that if she asked enough questions she would figure out the real reason why she was there. And if she figured out the real reason why she was there, she would bolt. Subpoena or no subpoena. As Damien told me, his mother was very unpredictable and was not afraid of being arrested. That meant she would have no problems at all jumping. I had to keep her in the courthouse, so the less contact I had with her, the better.

Damien was in the courtroom, waiting for me. "Do you think Mom will help or hurt me?"

"Damien, if I thought for a second she would hurt you, I wouldn't call her. Granted, I'm not positive she'll help you, but I have a good idea she probably will. The more we can show the jury other people who had it in both for you and Josh, the better off we'll be."

"I hope you're right. I don't want to sound like I'm doubtful of your abilities, because that's really not it. On the contrary, I'm very confident in your abilities. I guess I'm just nervous. My life is on the line and I don't like not knowing."

"Oh, I understand. Trust me, I understand."

Nick came in the courtroom and then the bailiff announced the judge was about to take her seat. The jury filed in and everybody was ready to go. The bailiff announced the case, Judge Grant banged her gavel, and the proceedings were underway.

It was time to get Olivia on the stand. I would have to break her down and she would hate me.

That is, if I did my job right.

"Ms. Ross," Judge Grant said. "Please call your first witness."

I cleared my throat. "The defense calls Olivia Ward."

The bailiff went out to get Olivia and she came in. I nodded as she passed by me but she gave me a look that told me she knew the real reason why she'd been called.

She didn't look happy. Not in the least.

She took her seat at the witness stand, was sworn in, stated her name, and I got to work.

"Ms. Ward," I began, "could you please tell the court your relationship to the accused?"

"I'm his mama."

"And what is your relationship to the deceased, Josh Roland?"

She rolled her eyes. "I ain't got no relationship to that man. Trust me, I ain't got no relationship to him."

"Be that as it may, Ms. Ward, you know the deceased, right?"

"I ain't been in touch with him. Not since he raped me years ago and knocked me up. He was my son's sperm donor. I guess that's the only relationship I have to him."

"So, it's fair to say you don't have much love for the deceased, Josh Roland, correct?"

She rolled her eyes. "Same answer I gave to you earlier. I told you I've got no relationship to him and that means I've got no relationship to him. So no, I have no love for that man."

"In fact, you hate him, right?"

"Hate is such a strong word. But yeah, I think the man's a bastard and a son of a bitch, to say the very least."

I noted in my head that things were going as well as I could possibly imagine. "Now, you mentioned something about Josh Roland raping you. Is it fair to say you're very angry with Mr. Roland for doing that to you?"

"Yeah," she said. "Listen, I know where you're going with this." She shook her head. "You lied to me. You said I would be a character witness. But that's not the truth. The reality is you're trying to throw me under the bus for Josh Roland's murder. I'm onto your game."

"That's not responsive to my question. My question is, are you angry with Mr. Roland?"

"Hell yes I'm angry with Mr. Roland. What do you think, after a man rapes you? You think I'm to going to become his poker buddy? Maybe take him out to brunch? Yeah, I don't like the guy. But I didn't kill him. I know where you're going with this."

I ignored her rant. I simply had to keep going and try to methodically break her down. "And what about your son, Damien?"

"What about him?"

"What is your relationship to him? Is it close? Or is it strained?"

"Listen, my son is too big for his britches if you ask me, and always has been. He's never been happy with the kind of life I've been able to give him. He's always been looking for greener pastures. And he found it. He went to law school and became a big-shot lawyer. Good for him. But he ain't wanted to have nothing to do with me, that's for sure. Not until recently."

I nodded. "Not until recently. What do you mean? What happened recently between you and Mr. Harrington?"

"Well he finally decided one day to grace me with his presence. He just showed up at my door one day, just like nothing had ever happened. Just like he never decided to stop returning my phone calls for years and years. We've been talking since then. I like his kids."

"You like his kids? What about Damien himself? Do you like him too?"

"I didn't kill Josh and frame Damien for his murder. I don't hate my son that much. Hell, I kinda like him these days. I don't feel like he judges me as much. God knows he's in no position to judge nobody at the moment." Then she laughed. I looked over at Damien and he just shook his head.

I felt like this direct examination of Olivia was going quite well. It was pretty obvious she had antipathy towards her son. Her antagonistic attitude towards Damien was obvious with every word she spoke.

"Ms. Ward," I said, "Damien actually established a relationship with his father recently, correct?"

She snorted. "If you could call it that. It was pretty much Damien trying to kiss his father's ass and his father not giving a crap."

"Why did Damien even try to establish a relationship with Josh?"

"I don't know. What are you getting at?"

"When you first told Damien who his father was, and how Damien was conceived, did Damien want to have anything to do with his father?"

"No. He didn't. I told Damien the Roland family was a bunch of freaks and weirdoes. Drug addicts, cray people, you name it. I don't think there's a good apple in that entire Roland barrel. Damien wanted nothing to do with Josh."

"Yet, Damien established a relationship with Josh. Why?"

It apparently just dawned on Olivia what I was driving at. "Oh, I see. Well, I let the cat out of the bag to Josh about the fact he had a son. Then I might've told Damien a little white lie." She put her thumb and forefinger together. "Just a little white lie."

"And what was that white lie?"

"I told Damien his father was a reformed man. I told Damien his father was in AA, was working his 1 2 steps, was on the step about making amends and wanted to make amends to me."

I nodded. "You lied to Damien. Why did you lie?"

"I guess because I decided I wanted Damien to know his father. That's all."

"I see. The father who was from a family of weirdoes and freaks? The father who raped and impregnated you? That father?"

"Yeah, that father. Listen, you don't always get to choose who gives you your genes. I never knew my dad. I wanted Damien to know his. That's all."

I paced back and forth, trying to lay my trap. "When you went to Josh to tell him he had a son, did he react with joy?"

She snorted again and shook her head. "God no. That bastard threatened me when I told him about Damien. Told me that if I tried to shake him down for money, he would kill me. Told me that if I told anybody about him raping me he would burn me alive. No, that news wasn't met with any kind of joy, I'll tell you that."

"So, it was fair to say the chances for a happy reunion between Damien and Josh wasn't good?"

"Yeah, that's fair. But Josh surprised me. When I told Damien, and Damien went to meet him, he was civil to Damien. Nice, even."

"Well, that was because Josh was obsessed with Damien's ex-wife, Sarah, right?"

"Yeah, I think that's right. Josh did his own ass-kissing to

Damien because he wanted to get close to Sarah. I think that's true."

"But you didn't think Josh would react well to meeting Damien, did you?"

"No, but a girl can hope, can't she? Listen, I never knew my dad. I never had a dad around. I felt bad that Damien didn't have a dad either. I figured that even a crazy sperm-donor like Josh was still a sperm-donor and Damien should at least get the chance to see if he could try to make nice with his dad. That's all."

I raised an eyebrow and paced around. "That's not all, though, was it? You set Damien up, didn't you? Set him up to take the fall for your plan to kill Josh?"

She looked at me for a few seconds and then burst out laughing. "Oh, lordy, you have a good imagination." She laughed some more. "Yeah, that's what I did – I sent my son to meet his dad just because I wanted to kill his dad and pin it on him. Yeah, that's right. I'm a master chess player like that. A puppet-master, yanking on everybody's strings. That's me."

She was still laughing, but I proceeded forward. "Ms. Ward, this is a serious matter. Frankly, from where I sit, I see the only reason why you would introduce Damien to Josh would be to frame him for a murder you were planning to commit. So, isn't it true that was the only reason why you encouraged Damien to meet his father?"

She shook her head and laughed some more. "No," she said. "That wasn't why. That's a good story, though. A really good story."

I figured I did my duty. I put reasonable doubt in the minds of the jury-members that maybe, just maybe, Olivia did it. I knew the evidence against her wasn't enough to charge her. Not at all. But the evidence I presented might've been enough to sow seeds of doubt in the jury members. That was all I was aiming for, and I thought I did my job. "I have nothing further."

"Mr. Wright, your witness."

Nick stood up and approached Olivia. "Ms. Ward, you didn't kill Josh and frame your son, did you?"

"No." She suppressed another giggle. "I didn't."

"I was just clarifying this, because you just told the jury you did kill Josh and frame Damien."

"I was joking. My God, can't you take a joke?"

Nick nodded his head. "And you encouraged Damien's relationship with his dad because you felt Damien needed a father figure in his life, correct?"

"Right."

"I have nothing further."

"Ms. Ross, any re-direct?"

"None, your honor."

"Ms. Ward, you may step down."

"Thank God," she said. "I need a drink. And a smoke."

I heard the jury laughing and I had to suppress my own laughter. Olivia was a card, that was for sure.

Olivia walked out of the courtroom and the judge ordered me to call my next witness.

"The defense calls Sarah White."

CHAPTER 31

The bailiff went to get Sarah, who was standing outside the courtroom, and she walked in. She had dyed her hair jet black, which actually was striking on her. With her pale skin and pale eyes, she looked almost like a Goth chick. She was wearing a lot more makeup than the last time I'd seen her as well.

She walked to the witness stand and sat down. She clasped her hands in front of her and looked at me with challenging eyes. The expression on her face said *I'm here, what you gonna do about it.* I knew one thing. Sarah wouldn't play dumb. I didn't think she was like Olivia, who was either playing dumb was kind of dumb. I couldn't tell which scenario was true. But with Sarah, I knew she would answer my questions, with attitude.

Sarah was sworn in, and I asked her name for the record.

"Sarah White," she said.

"Ms. White, you've been called to testify in the case against Damien Harrington. Could you please tell the court how you are related to Mr. Harrington?"

"Mr. Harrington is my ex-husband."

"Your ex-husband? When did the two of you divorce?"

"About six months ago. He filed for divorce last spring and it was finalized in the early fall."

"Was the split friendly?"

She scoffed. "No, it wasn't friendly. It wasn't friendly at all. He basically told me one day I needed to get out. I thought we were working on our marriage, we were going to give it a shot. We were going to marriage counseling, even. He decided out of the blue he wanted to end it. So no, it wasn't friendly."

"The two of you have children, correct?"

"Yes, that's right."

"Two children?"

"Yes, Nate and Amelia."

"Do you have a relationship with your children?"

She looked over at Nick, wanting him to object. I know what she was thinking. She was wondering what the relevance was of my asking her these questions and why she was even called to testify in the first place. I somehow thought she was naïve and didn't really know the reason why I wanted her to testify today. I felt bad about that, but it was what it was.

Nick finally did stand up. "Objection," he said. "Lack of relevance."

Judge Grant looked at me. "Ms. Ross, what is the relevance of this line of questioning?"

"Your honor, as I was stating in my opening statements, I need to show this witness had reason to be angry with Damien. Since my theory of the case is that somebody killed Josh and framed Damien, I need to show the possibility that this witness did the crime. So I have to show their split was acrimonious."

"I'll allow it," Judge Grant said. "Proceed."

I looked back at Sarah and she was staring daggers at me. My earlier hunch might've been correct. It was possible she didn't really know why she was called to testify. If she didn't know why before, she certainly did now.

"Ms. White, please answer the question."

She swallowed hard. Her hands fidgeted in front of her. "I live in Chicago now."

I nodded. "So, because you live in Chicago, is it fair to say you don't have a relationship with your children?"

"That's what I'm saying. I never see my children."

"Ms. White, what are your feelings towards my client, Damien Harrington?"

"I don't have any feelings for him right now. None at all."

"But Ms. White, you told the court earlier he ended it, and when he ended it, he blindsided you. The two of you were married for over 10 years, correct?"

"Yes, that's correct."

"And so your testimony is that even though he just asked you to leave one day, when you thought things were going fine, you don't have any feelings for him at all?"

"That's my testimony." She looked over Damien and glared.

I nodded. She wasn't credible and everybody knew it. At least anybody with eyes knew it. Anybody who could see her, staring at her ex-husband, with hate in her eyes, knew the truth. And then she looked at me with just as much hatred. That was okay, I welcomed her hatred.

If she hated me, it meant I was doing my job.

"I would like to move onto your relationship with the deceased, Josh Roland. When was the first time you encountered Mr. Roland?"

"When I was a young girl. 10 years old."

"When you were 10 years old? How did you come to know him when you were 10 years old?"

"He hired my father to build some apartment buildings downtown. He hired him individually, not his company."

"Your father, what did he do?"

"He owned a construction company. He was a general contractor."

"A general contractor. So, he made a contract with Josh Roland?"

"Yes. That's right." She looked down at her hands. I saw a look in her eye that was very sad. At that point, I started to feel guilty about what I was about to do. I had to suck it up though. Damien's life depended on it.

"Do you know how much the contract was for?"

She nodded her head. "Yes. According to the contract, Josh Roland was supposed to pay my father $1 million to build this apartment building."

"$1 million? That's a lot of money isn't it?"

"I guess." She shrugged her shoulders.

"Do you know how much money your father put into these apartment buildings?"

"Yes. He put $200,000 into it."

"$200,000. How big was this company?"

"Not very big. He only had 10 employees. Most of the work he did was through subcontractors. It was a small company but it was a thriving one."

"Do you know how your father felt to get a contract with a man like Josh Roland?"

She nodded. Again, her expression was very sad. "He was very excited. I remember he came home after making the contract and he and my mom were dancing around the room. He thought his ship had come in. He thought that contract with Josh Roland would make his business explode. He imagined that if he did a good job, Mr. Roland would tell all his wealthy friends about my dad's company, and we would all be millionaires within a few years. That's what he thought would happen. He took us all out to an expensive steak dinner at the Hereford House the night he got the contract. I had never seen him so happy."

As she spoke, I had a feeling of dread. I knew how the story ended. And hearing her speak about what happened when her father made a contract with Josh Roland made me want to burst into tears myself. It was as if I was watching a movie that started out happy and ended in great tragedy. It was a roller coaster. Somehow, hearing just how thrilled her father was to be contracting with Josh Roland made this story even more poignant. And powerful. I knew her telling the story would make her look like she had good cause to murder Josh. That was what I was aiming for yet I couldn't help but feel very sorry for her.

"Is that what happened?" I asked softly. "Did your father's company boom after he contracted with Josh Roland? Did Mr. Roland pass your father's name around to his wealthy friends after your father's company built that apartment complex?"

She shifted uncomfortably in her seat. "No. That's not what happened."

"What did happen?"

She sighed. "My father had great business skills. But he was a little naïve. He had a blind spot when it came to this particular person, Josh Roland. When they made the contract, my father agreed to put up all the money needed to be put up for the apartment complex, in exchange for getting the $1 million on the back end. So, my father hired all the subcontractors, paid his employees and supplied all the materials for the complex. He did everything according to the contract. He had building inspectors come in and the apartment complex was approved by everybody who came to inspect it. I saw the apartment complex myself, and it was beautiful. Absolutely beautiful. Of course, I was only 10 years old, but it looked very nice to me. And there was nothing wrong with it. Nothing at all."

"Okay, so he built the apartment complex, putting up all the money, and not getting any money up front from Mr. Roland? Is that what you're saying?"

She nodded her head. "Yes, that's what I'm saying."

"And did Josh Roland hold up his end of the bargain?"

She shook her head. I could see tears in her eyes. "No. Mr. Roland called my father and told him the apartment complex was made with shoddy workmanship, and would not pay my father a dime." She swallowed hard and shook her head back and forth. "He refused to pay on the contract."

"So, your father outlayed all this money, time and resources, and didn't get paid at all by Josh Roland. Is that what you're saying?"

"Yes, that's what I'm saying."

"How did your father react when Mr. Roland refused payment?"

"My father was not a very volatile man. He didn't lose his temper very much. He was pretty practical, so the first thing he did was hire an attorney."

"Did the attorney file a lawsuit?"

"He did. He filed a lawsuit."

"And what happened with that lawsuit?"

Sarah gritted her teeth. "What happened with that lawsuit was that Mr. Roland had a team of lawyers on his side and his lawyers bombarded my father's lawyers with discovery request after discovery request. They asked for reams of documents. They sent one interrogatory after another. Now, I was only 10 years old at the time, so I didn't understand what was happening. As an adult, I found out what happened with that lawsuit. And I understood why my father ended up finally dropping the suit. He couldn't pay his attorney, because Mr. Roland's attorneys just kept coming with one thing after another. You have to understand, my father had just lost $200,000. His business wasn't that big to begin with. He didn't have that much cash on hand after he lost that money. He couldn't pay that attorney. So, he ended up dropping the lawsuit against Mr. Roland."

"What happened after he ended up dropping that lawsuit?"

She sighed. "He filed for bankruptcy and went to work for a construction company making $15 an hour. My mother didn't work. My brother was sick with cancer at the time, so she couldn't work. She had to be there for him. So, my father was trying to make ends meet with three children, one who was sick in the hospital, and he just couldn't. He couldn't make ends meet. I remember that Christmas, he came home to tell us kids that Santa couldn't come to our house that year. I didn't believe in Santa Claus at that time anyway, but my little sister did. I never forgot the look in her eyes as she realized Santa Claus couldn't bring her anything she wanted that year. And I can never get the look in my father's eyes out of my head. I will never forget how he looked when he told the three of us there couldn't be any Christmas that year for us."

"What else happened?"

"Well we were living in a nice house in Lee's Summit. It wasn't a mansion, but it was big enough for all of us. But after my father lost that money, he lost his business, had to file for bankruptcy, and owed a lot of attorney's bills too. He would have to sell the house to try to get caught up with some of his debts. The five of us started looking at two-bedroom apartments. I didn't know how that would work, there were three of us kids, but that was how it would be. All at once, we went from being a solid middle-class family to almost being on the streets."

"And this was all because of Josh, correct?"

"Yes." She nodded her head. "If Mr. Roland would have

at least paid the money my father had outlayed on the apartment complex, my father could've made it work. But he refused to pay anything. My father lost his business, his home, and his will to live." She swallowed hard. "My father killed himself that Christmas Eve. I read the suicide note. My mom didn't know I had read it, but I did. The note said he was sorry but he knew he couldn't provide for us. He wrote that he felt like life wasn't worth living because he was a man who couldn't provide for his family anymore. That was why he killed himself. My brother died a few months later."

As I looked in her face, I felt a burning hatred for Josh Roland. I felt she hated him, but I hated him as well. What kind of man would do something like that? What kind of a man would destroy the life of an entire family just because he's greedy, selfish and corrupt? For that reason, and so many more, I really felt it was justice that Josh died the way he did.

"Now, I would like to bring you to the present day. You went to work for Josh, isn't that right?"

"Yes."

"What did you do for him?"

"I'm a kindergarten teacher. I have the summers off. I went to work for him one summer. I was his assistant."

"By assistant, what do you mean? What were your job duties?"

"I handled some of his charity work. Specifically, I lined up charitable functions for him, and I also made charitable donations to people and organizations. I also worked with his investments, entering them into a computer."

"What was the real reason you went to work for him?"

"I wanted access to his financial records. I wanted to look for any kind of irregularities, and if I found any, I would put them on an external hard drive and turn that hard drive over to the authorities. That was why I really went to work for him. I wanted to bring him down."

This was going very well. I knew she would be forthcoming on the stand, mainly because of the penalty for perjury. But I think it was also cathartic for her to say out loud what her scheme was for Josh Roland. I think she wanted the jury to know she had revenge in mind when she worked for him.

Not that I blamed her.

Nobody would.

"You wanted to bring him down. Was that your plan? Was it only you who planned this?"

"No. I planned it but so did Olivia."

"Olivia Ward, Damien's mom, right?"

"Yes, Olivia Ward."

"So did the plan go forward? Did you find the information you were looking for?"

"Yes, I did. I found evidence he was involved in insider trading. I found firm evidence of this."

"And did you put that evidence on a hard drive, and turn it into the authorities?"

She shook her head. "No, I didn't."

"And why not?"

She sighed. "Because he raped me one day in his office, and I knew I couldn't ever go back into that office again. He also impregnated me and I had an abortion. That baby could very well have been my husband's child, but I didn't know for sure, so I aborted the baby. I destroyed a life because of him. That makes me sick. He makes me sick."

I didn't blame her there. Josh made me sick too. But I soldiered on. "So, is it safe to say you hate Josh Roland?"

"Oh, I do. I do. And I'm not afraid to say I thought justice was served when the guy was murdered. He was hurting far too many people. But I wasn't the one who gave him that justice.

Was I cheering and clapping when I found out Josh been bludgeoned in his office? Yes I was. I was. I would've been very disappointed if he had died without suffering, like if somebody had slipped something in his drink and he just went to sleep and never woke up. But he was beaten to death, which meant he suffered. And yes, I believe that was just rewards. I won't lie about that. I wish I did it myself but I didn't."

I nodded. I felt I had gone as far as I could with her and there was nothing more to ask her. "I have nothing further for this witness."

As I looked at her knew I didn't feel good about what I did to her. I didn't feel good about making her relive all those bad memories. I didn't feel good about making the jury think she killed Josh. However, I thought that maybe she didn't mind if the jury thought she killed him. As with Olivia, there was no way the authorities would have enough on Sarah to charge her with anything. It was all circumstantial evidence. Yet I knew her testimony had put doubt into the jury's minds and that's all I wanted. I also thought her testimony on the stand actually was good for her. It allowed her to get all her hatred and rage out for all the world to see. So maybe I did her a favor.

At least I hoped so.

"Mr. Wright, your witness," Judge Grant said.

Nick stood up and straightened his tie. Then he sat down. "I have nothing for this witness."

Judge Grant nodded and then banged her gavel. "Okay, it's time for a break." She looked at the clock. "It is now 2:15. I'm going to let all of you take a short 10 minute break. Well, let's make it a 15 minute break. Everybody be back here by 2:30." At that, she turned and walked off the bench.

As the jury filed out of the room, I looked over at Damien. "How did that go? How did you feel about my examination of Sarah?"

He shrugged. "You know, I never even knew how affected she was by everything that happened to her when she was a kid. It's times like this that I really feel bad for her. I mean, we've had our problems, and I would never let her back into my life, but I do feel sorry for her. She lost her father in such a way and her brother a few months later. And the fact that Josh Roland was behind all of...." He shook his head. "That man was a bastard and Sarah was right about one thing – he deserved what he got."

"I know he deserved what he got. At this point, I don't think there's any disputing that. Some people just need to be killed and Josh was one of them. The good thing is that, at least with your wife and Olivia, I don't think there would ever be enough evidence to charge them with Josh's murder. But I think I'm putting doubt in the minds of the jury, so that's a good thing."

"A very good thing. So what do you think? How do you think things are going?"

"Pretty good. I think I showed that both Olivia and Sarah had reason to kill Josh, and I hope I also showed they had reason to frame you. I also think Olivia's not that mad about being brought in here and thrown under the bus. So that's a good thing."

"Yeah. My mom and I have been trying to mend our fences and we were slowly starting to get to know one another. My kids love her so I want a relationship with her. I think you're right – I think my mom probably is not too upset about being brought in here and questioned. I don't think it'll cause a problem between the two of us."

A few minutes later, the jury came back in and so did the judge. She rapped her gavel on the bench and addressed the jury. "Okay, ladies and gentlemen of the jury, I hope you had a nice break. We're going to resume the case of State vs. Harrington. I'll remind you the defense is now presenting her case and the defense needs to call her next witness." She nodded at me. "Okay, Ms. Ross, please call your next witness."

This next witness was actually the one I actually really wanted to talk to.

It was the first lady of Missouri, Addison Weston.

CHAPTER 32

"The defense calls Addison Weston," I announced.

The bailiff went out and got Mrs. Weston. She appeared in the courtroom, walking slowly. She was dressed in a Chanel suit, hose, and white pumps. Her hair was perfectly coiffed in a short blonde bob. She was carrying a Birkin bag that was probably worth more than my entire car and her makeup was done perfectly. She was an attractive woman. She wasn't very tall, around five foot five, and probably weighed less than hundred and twenty pounds.

She took her seat behind the witness stand, putting in her purse on the stand. She looked me in the eye and I knew she was curious as to why she was there. But she shouldn't have been. I had my suspicions she was the one who actually did this. I just hoped I could bring it out on the stand.

The bailiff swore her in and I approached.

"Could you please state your name for the record?"

She leaned forward into the microphone. "Addison Marie Weston."

"And Miss Weston, you're married to Governor John Weston. Is that correct?"

"It is."

"Ms. Weston, that means you are the First Lady of the State of Missouri. Is that correct?"

"Yes, that is correct." Her posture was perfectly straight and I could tell she wouldn't give me anything more than what I asked her. Her answers would be short and sweet and I would have to draw her out. That was fine. I was up to the challenge.

"Now Ms. Weston, you're married to the governor of the State of Missouri, but you actually were going to file for divorce from him, correct?"

"Yes I was."

"But you haven't actually filed for divorce, have you?"

"No, I have not."

"Permission to treat as hostile." I wanted to do that preemptively, as I wanted to ask leading questions. Ordinarily on direct, you cannot ask leading questions. But if you treat the witness as hostile, you can. Usually you had to wait for the person to lie to treat them as hostile. But I hoped the judge would give me leeway to do it.

"Permission granted." I guessed the judge was curious about what the governor's wife would say as much as anybody else so she wanted to make sure I could examine her with ease.

"Isn't it true that you haven't filed for divorce because you were hopeful for a decent settlement, but you couldn't get that?"

"Well, yes. I definitely was trying to get a good settlement out of my husband." She put her hand on the back of her neck and rubbed.

"But is it true you couldn't get the settlement because something damaging was not made public because Damien covered up a piece of information about your husband that would've given you leverage over him?"

She looked uncomfortable. "Yes, that's true."

"Isn't it true the piece of information you wanted was an obscene picture that your husband, Governor Weston, sent to a young artist?"

"Yes, that's true."

"And that picture was not made public because Damien and your husband conspired to make it private. Isn't that true?"

"Yes." She started look kind of upset. "Yes, that's true. If my husband and Mr. Harrington did not make that agreement, that picture would've been public. And my husband would've been humiliated. He would've been humiliated, and I would've gotten anything I wanted from him. That's because if that picture would've been made public the whole world would've known my husband is a pervert who likes boys."

I was surprised she was so forthcoming. Yet I knew it was a good thing.

"So, is it safe to say you're angry with my client, Damien Harrington?"

"I don't even know him."

"That's not the question I asked. I asked if you're angry with my client, Damien Harrington?"

She looked at Damien and I could see hatred in her eyes. "Yes, I'm angry with him. I don't know him, but I do blame him for the fact I couldn't get the settlement I wanted in my divorce."

"Now, I would like to turn your attention to the victim in this case, Josh Roland. You knew him, didn't you?"

"Yes, I did. I knew him."

"And, isn't it true you knew him because the two of you were having an affair?"

She shifted in her seat. Then she looked me right in the eye. "Yes, I was having an affair with Mr. Roland."

"And isn't it true you thought you would marry him? Actually, isn't that another reason why you decided not to divorce your husband? Because you thought you would marry Mr. Roland, but you found out he was not as serious about you as you were about him?"

She got closer to the microphone. "Yes, that's true. I was in love with him. But then I found he not only didn't love me back but was not even serious about me. I found out he was having affairs with numerous women."

"And didn't you also find out about his sexual predation?"

She blinked, and I saw tears in her eyes. "Yes, I did. I don't know how, but somebody found out I was having an affair with him and wanted to marry him. When that knowledge became known in certain circles, I started having visitors to my office. There were young women who would tell me their stories about what Josh did to them. One woman after another came to me in confidence to tell me that Mr. Roland was harassing them. Each of them swore me to secrecy."

"And isn't it true that because of what you found out about Josh, you've made the issue of sexual harassment your pet cause?" Ironically, Addison Weston was the leading advocate for women and girls who were being harassed in the State of Missouri. She had made many speeches about this within the past year. She had advocated for increased funding for the Attorney General to go after sexual harassment cases in the government.

"Yes, that's true. I found out what Mr. Roland was doing and it made me sick. Yes, that's true. I've been a leading advocate for women and girls who have faced predators such as him."

Now it was time to lay my trap. "Now, isn't it true you wanted to surveil Mr. Roland?"

She took a deep breath. She knew where this was going, and I think she knew she was caught. At least, as I looked into her eyes, I saw fear.

"Yes, I did wanted him surveilled."

"And the reason why you wanted him surveilled was because you wanted the girls and women he was harassing to be believed. Isn't that correct?"

"I thought it was disgraceful, just disgraceful, that he was doing all this to people and getting away with it. I knew most of the women and girls who came to see me said they'd told people about what he was doing but nobody would believe them. I thought that was just terrible. So yes, I wanted some kind of proof for these women and girls."

"And you sent him a lamp, didn't you? You sent him this lamp as an anonymous gift?"

"Yes. I bought him that lamp. I sent it as an anonymous gift, but it really shouldn't have been anonymous. There should've been a clue it came from me because it was an Oriental lamp. Josh and I had traveled the Far East together when I thought we were in love. So I bought him that lamp, thinking he'd know it was from me."

"And the reason why you gave him that lamp was because you'd implanted surveillance equipment in there. Isn't that true?"

I was getting excited. I really didn't know she had bought him that lamp - I just had a feeling. But I was very surprised to admit to it. And I was also surprised she admitted she wanted Josh to be surveilled. It made sense she would want him to be surveilled, but I never imagined she actually would admit to it. I was asking questions in the dark and was hitting gold.

"Yes. That's true. That was the reason why I bought him that lamp."

"And isn't it true that because you bought that lamp and were in charge of the surveillance equipment, you knew that my client, Damien Harrington, had threatened Mr. Roland with that very lamp?"

She blinked her eyes at me. I had her, and she knew it. But did I think she actually beat Josh up with that lamp? No. I didn't think that. However, I thought she had somebody working for Josh, and instructed that person, whoever it was, to kill Josh with that lamp. That was the only thing that made sense to me, considering the First Lady was in Jefferson City at the time of the murder. She must've thought that it was great luck that her lamp surveillance equipment recorded Damien threatening Josh with that very lamp. She hated Damien because she felt Damien was responsible for her not getting the information she needed to bring down her husband. And she hated Josh. She placed the surveillance equipment in that lamp.

I knew then that she was responsible for killing Josh.

I just had to sell that story to the jury.

"Yes, I did find that out."

"And isn't it true you hired somebody to monitor Josh? Somebody working for him?"

My heart stopped as I suddenly realized who probably was behind this. Jacqueline Peterson. That would make sense, considering the testimony she'd given to the police about Damien.

The First Lady shifted uncomfortably in her chair. "Yes, that's true. I did hire somebody to monitor Josh. I wanted him to be surveilled, and I also wanted someone close to him to make sure he stayed in line."

I suddenly knew I would have to look into Jacqueline Peterson's finances and find out if a large deposit had been made in her bank account recently. I thought about calling her to the stand again, but I wasn't sure about her. I only had a hunch. And I had a very big hunch the First Lady was behind it. She hired somebody, probably Jacqueline Peterson, to kill Josh.

"Was that somebody Jacqueline Peterson by any chance?"

She knew she could not lie on the stand. It would be easy enough to find out that Jacqueline Peterson was the person she hired.

"Yes. I hired Jacqueline Peterson."

CHAPTER 33

Bingo. "So you hired Jacqueline Peterson to essentially spy on Mr. Roland."

"Yes, that's essentially what Jacqueline Peterson did for me."

"Isn't it true you saw an opportunity to have Jacqueline Peterson do more than just spy on Mr. Roland? Specifically, you heard my client threatening Mr. Roland with that lamp. And you knew that was an opportunity to send Jacqueline Peterson into Mr. Roland's office and bludgeon him with that lamp. Isn't that true?"

Her fingers suddenly flew up to her throat and she yanked on her necklace. She turned very white. I knew I had her. With a shaky voice, she said, "No. No, that's not what happened."

I started pacing around. I had her on the run. "Oh? Is that not what happened? You were angry with my client, because you blamed him, irrationally, for torpedoing your divorce settlement. And you're angry with Josh for not returning your affections. Not only that, but you found out what kind of person he was. That made you sick. Admit it, you could not believe your luck when you picked up my client threatening Josh Roland with that lamp. You knew it was your opportunity to send Jacqueline Peterson into the office to bludgeon Josh Roland to death with that lamp. Admit it."

Her fingers went to her hair. She was shaking all over. She shook her head, again and again. "I plead the Fifth. I plead the Fifth."

I nodded. "I have nothing further for this witness."

I sat down, feeling relieved. I got what I needed out of that witness. And I knew I would have to change my closing arguments. And from that point on, this case would be a cakewalk. Unfortunately, the governor's wife would be questioned by the authorities. I felt bad for her. After all, she did the world a favor by having that bastard killed. She really should've gotten a medal for that one. I was sure she would find a good lawyer and plead some kind of insanity or something like that. Or maybe even try for outright acquittal. I didn't know.

What I did know was the case, in my mind, it was over.

What I found out later was that Nick Wright also knew the case was over. After Addison Weston was dismissed from the stand, Nick Wright stood up and asked to take a five-minute break.

Judge Grant said, "I'll do you one better than that, let's take a half-hour break. I'd like to see both of you in my chambers. The jury is dismissed for now, but be back in a half hour."

The judge disappeared from behind the bench and Nick and I went through the doors to go to the judge's chambers.

"Have a seat," Judge Grant said, and Nick and I sat down. "Mr. Wright, I think you and I both know where this case is going. Are you going to dismiss it?"

Nick shook his head. "No, I think we still have a shot. I don't want to dismiss it."

Judge Grant rolled her eyes. "At this point, it's a waste of taxpayer's dollars to keep going. We both know who did it and it wasn't Damien Harrington. You saw that woman on the stand. Same as me. And when she pled the Fifth, that was it for me. Now I'm inclined to do a Directed Verdict, but I would prefer for you to dismiss the case." She looked over at me. "Too many Directed Verdicts look bad. I won't lie."

"I don't think Jacqueline Peterson did it. There was only one set of fingerprints on that lamp, besides Mr. Harrington's," Nick protested.

"Ms. Peterson wore gloves. It was cold outside that week. I remember," I said.

"There weren't any glove prints on the murder weapon," Nick said.

"So, the cops missed it. They didn't do a dusting for glove prints. It wouldn't be the first time the cops did a shitty job processing a crime scene and it won't be the last," I said.

Judge Grant raised an eyebrow at Nick. "You dismiss it or I will. Your choice."

Nick look defeated, but the handwriting was on the wall.

Judge Grant smiled. "Don't look so depressed about this. You'll get your chance to prosecute somebody for the death of Josh Roland. I fully believe Jacqueline Peterson's case will be coming to trial sooner than you think. Not to mention Addison Weston." Judge Grant shook her head. "That'll be a shit show. The circus will be coming to town on that one, if it goes to trial. I just hope I'm not the Emcee." She chuckled. "Imagine that, a First Lady up for murder. So cheer up, Mr. Wright. If you play your cards right, you might be prosecuting Addison Weston for the murder. A high-profile case like that could make your career. Look at Marcia Clark. She's still riding that gravy train."

I looked over at Nick and saw he knew she was right. If he got the chance to prosecute the First Lady for murder, that really could make his career. That was a good consolation prize for him.

"Okay, I'll dismiss the case."

"Good call," Judge Grant said. "Okay, then. We're on the same page. Now you just go out there and dismiss the case on the record. With prejudice. And then we can all go home."

We all went into the courtroom. The jury was already there waiting for us.

Judge Grant looked at Nick. "Mr. Wright, do you have any motions for me?"

Nick stood up. "I move to dismiss all charges against Mr. Harrington, with prejudice."

Judge Grant nodded her head and banged her gavel. "It is so ordered." Then she looked over at the jury. "I'm sorry ladies and gentlemen, for wasting your time. We do appreciate your time and service, but you're free to go."

I looked over at Damien, and he was laughing. He shook his head.

"You can't make this stuff up," he said.

I was laughing too. "No, you can't."

CHAPTER 35
NOVEMBER 6

Jacqueline Peterson was working at Aragon International when she saw Damien Harrington come into the suite. He smiled pleasantly at her. "I'm here to see Mr. Roland," he said.

Jacqueline thought that was unusual as she didn't have him on the schedule. But she also knew Damien was Mr. Roland's son, and, from what she knew, Mr. Roland wanted to get to know Damien. And Damien happened to come at a time when Mr. Roland didn't have meetings. She figured it couldn't hurt to let Damien in unannounced.

"Just a second," she said. "I'll buzz Mr. Roland." She called him on the phone, and he said Damien could come back for a short visit. She looked up at him. "He said he has a few minutes to speak with you. You can go on in."

About a half-hour later, Damien emerged from Mr. Roland's office. He looked slightly agitated. "Thanks for letting go back there. I'll show myself out."

He left and then she got a phone call. From Addison Weston.

"Hello, Mrs. Weston," Jacqueline said. "How are you?"

"Fine. Listen, I know that we have an arrangement, but how would you like to make an easy million dollars?"

Jacqueline's ears perked up. She had a lot of gambling debts and was on the verge of filing for bankruptcy and losing her home. "What do I need to do?"

"Listen, we have an opportunity of a lifetime. I just heard Damien Harrington threaten Mr. Roland. From what I could hear, Damien had that new lamp in his hands and was swinging it at Mr. Roland. I heard Mr. Roland scream 'put that lamp down,' and then I heard Damien say 'I could kill you.' Go in and check on Mr. Roland. See if he's okay. And if he is okay, go in there, with a pair of gloves, and bludgeon him with that lamp. Damien will be blamed for it because his fingerprints are obviously on that lamp. It'll be the perfect crime."

"What are you talking about?" Jacqueline asked. "I can't just go in and kill Mr. Roland."

"You can't? Do you remember why you started working for that bastard in the first place? Why you agreed to spy on him for me? Do you remember?"

Jacqueline took a deep breath. "I do."

"He raped your sister, didn't he? Now she's in and out of drug rehab, when, before he got ahold of her, she was going to Harvard. She dropped out of Harvard and became a junkie because of him. Don't forget that. That man hurts people. A lot of people. You'll be doing the world a favor if you get rid of him. But you have to do it now. Everybody has seen Damien come into the office. If you do it much later, the time of death won't coincide with when Damien was in there. Do it now. Do it now, and you'll be set for life."

"But I don't have anything against Damien. I hardly know him."

"Damien is a bastard, too, trust me on this. Do it. Do it. It'll be the perfect crime."

Jacqueline thought about it and then looked at the picture of her sister. She and her sister were on the tennis team together. In that picture, they looked so happy. This was before the rape. Before Amber started spiraling into heroin addiction. She used drugs to numb the pain of being violated like that. She had everything. She was going to be a doctor. Now, she could barely face life. She had been in and out of rehab five times, and, every day, Jacqueline was terrified she would get THAT call. The call about Amber being found dead in the street.

And Jacqueline *could* use the money. She would be set for life. She could help her sister out, too. Her sister had used up her insurance for all of her rehabs, so now, when she went to rehab, it was in a crappy state-run place. Jacqueline could use that million dollars to put Amber in a really good rehab facility, someplace where Amber could kick the drugs for good. And, Jacqueline thought, she could pay off her gambling debts and save her house.

And Addison was right. Mr. Roland didn't deserve to live. He hurt so many people. So many people.

"Okay, I'll do it."

Jacqueline hung up the phone, got her winter gloves out of her drawer, and went into Mr. Roland's office.

He was sitting at his desk and barely looked up when Jacqueline rushed towards him, picked up his Chinese lamp, and, before Mr. Roland knew what had happened, smashed it into his skull.

CHAPTER 34

After Damien and I left the courthouse, Damien asked if I could go over and see his mom with him. "I have a feeling we'll have to do some butt kissing."

"I agree. Let's go."

We went to her trailer house and she was there smoking a cigarette in her living room. As usual. She looked at the two of us as we walked through the door. "Well, come on in. Don't be shy."

"Mom, I wanted to talk to you about what happened today," Damien said.

"What, you mean how this one got me to testify on the stand and then proceeded to throw me under the bus? Is that what you wanted to talk to me about?" She shook her head. "That was a dirty trick. A really dirty trick." And then she laughed. "I should be pissed you thought I would do something like that to you and Josh. Well, I would've liked to have done something like that to Josh. He got what was coming to him. And trust me, I wish I swung that lamp at him and crushed his skull like a pumpkin after Halloween. But I didn't do it."

"I know. Harper thought you did it because she didn't see any other reason why you would want me to get to know my dad."

Olivia shook her head. "Well, that was a big mistake, I can see that now. That caused all this goddamned trouble. But I really did want you to know him. I never knew my dad and I always regretted that. I figured that, even if your dad was a nutjob, he was still your dad, so I wanted you to know him. That's all."

Damien smiled. "And we know you didn't kill Josh. Addison Weston, the First Lady of Missouri, all but admitted on the stand she was responsible for the murder."

Olivia laughed. "You gotta be kidding me. That prissy-priss did it? I didn't think she had it in her. She's so little. You mean to tell me she swung that lamp at him and killed him?"

"Well, she hired somebody to do it," Damien said.

Olivia shook her head. "Figures. She wouldn't get her hands dirty. So, I guess that's it, huh? You're a free man again, Damien?"

"Yeah." Damien paused. "We good?"

Olivia shrugged. "As good as we were before, I guess. Ah, I was pissed at first about you dragging me into this and trying to make the jury think I did it. But I figured I had it coming. I was shitty to you for a long time, Damien. I guess I don't really blame you for doing that." Then she shook her finger at both of us. "Just don't do it again."

I laughed. "Don't worry, we won't."

Damien soon got back to work, and his first client back was, of all people, Heather. Well, not really Heather, but her boyfriend, Beck Harrison. He was being accused of murdering a transgendered friend of Heather's. Yet, when Heather came into see Damien about hiring him, parts of her story just wasn't adding up. She showed up in his office and it was evident she'd been crying.

"Hey," he said to her. "Heather, what's going on?"

She just shook her head. "It's my boyfriend, Beck. He's been accused of something terrible. I don't know what to think. He says he didn't do it and I think I believe him. I don't know." She looked up at me. "I want you to represent him."

He rubbed my hands together. "What about Harper? How come you don't want her to represent him?"

Heather rolled her eyes. "Beck don't like women representing him. He thinks women aren't aggressive enough. Shhh, don't tell Harper that, though. She'd be pissed."

"Come on in my office," he said. "Let's get some facts together, and I can go and visit Beck. I'm assuming he's in jail?"

Heather nodded. "He is. God, he couldn't have done this. I just know he didn't do this."

He got out a yellow pad and paper. "What is he accused of doing?"

"He's accused of killing one of my sisters. By sister, I mean not actual sister, but another transgendered woman. They're charging it as a hate crime, which means they're gonna try for the death penalty."

No rest for the weary.

Do you want to know what happens next? Order *Hate Crime* for only $4.99

Description of *The Hate Crime*

A white supremacist charged with murdering a transgendered woman. A case where nobody is as they seem. A shocking 11th hour twist that changes the entire case.

Heather's back!

Heather Morrison is back in Damien's office, but this time, she's not just there to work. Her boyfriend, Beck Harrison, is accused of killing a transgendered friend of Heather's. The prosecutors are charging the murder as a hate crime. Beck insists he's innocent. After investigating Beck's background, Damien's not so sure. Beck has a dark past of involvement with the Aryan Brotherhood. But Damien soon finds out that this case is nothing like it seems. The victim's past soon becomes the target of the investigation, as Damien finds the one key that will break this case wide open.

Did Damien solve the crime or was there somebody else he never even thought of who might have been the culprit? A surprise witness at the 11th hour provides the clue.

Meanwhile, Connor has his own case for Damien. He's been working with underprivileged youth, trying to steer them straight and not walk the same path he has. He presses Damien to represent Tina, who is charged with drug distribution. Damien sees many parallels between Tina's life and his own, and he can't help wanting to save her.

But can he?

With the twists and turns you've come to expect in a Rachel Sinclair legal thriller, "The Hate Crime" is not to be missed!

https://amzn.to/2V9HMTx

For information about upcoming titles in the *Harper Ross Legal Thriller* series, sign up for my mailing list! You'll be the first to know about new releases and you'll be the first to know about any promotions!!!! https://mailchi.mp/2e2dda532e99/rachel-sinclair-legal-thrillers